KATE

&

RUBY

Emily Gallo

Cover design by Cody Vierra

The author may be reached at ecegallo@gmail.com
http://emilygallo.blogspot.com/

ISBN-13: 978-1950561049
ISBN-10: 1533361207

Other novels by Emily Gallo:

VENICE BEACH

THE COLUMBARIUM

"Life is what happens when you're busy making other plans."

John Lennon

Acknowledgements

I want to thank many people for their input; sometimes they have no clue that they have given me an idea that has grown into a character trait or a plot point. I want to give special appreciation to my outstanding editors, Chris Saur and Daniel Nauman.

1

"WAKE UP! THE LIGHT'S GREEN! THE GAS PEDAL IS ON THE RIGHT!" Maybe it was growing up in New York where everyone was always in a hurry. Or maybe it was living in Los Angeles for all those years, but she had no patience for drivers who took forever to accelerate when the light turned green. Were they texting, daydreaming, or were they just that slow on the uptake? She had lived in this idyllic northern California town for several years now, but maybe you just can't take the city out of the girl, or whatever that iconic expression was. She hated being late, even though her friends wouldn't care. They'd have already started in on a bottle of wine, even though it was her retirement, not theirs, they were celebrating. She still couldn't believe the day had finally come. She was a thin, fit, spry fifty-five year-old who looked like she hadn't aged in fifteen years. It also helped that she made sure there wasn't a gray strand anywhere in her pixie hairstyle.

She parked a couple of blocks away from the restaurant. She didn't want to have to pay the valet and besides, she would probably welcome a couple of blocks walk after eating and drinking more than she wanted. She loved her friends dearly, but they were much more the partying type than she. These dinners, even when they weren't celebrating anything in particular, always left her stomach stuffed, her head spinning, and her wallet empty.

The hostess brought her to a back room in the restaurant. She thought it odd since there were several empty tables in the main dining room, but maybe her friends had asked for an especially quiet place. When she walked into the room, however, her heart sank. There were many more people than the two women she had expected. And the banner hanging from the ceiling read "GOOD LUCK KATE". Shit! The last thing she had wanted was a retirement party with every single school employee and even some that had already left. She hated these kinds of rituals and ceremonies. This was not going to be a fun evening. She glanced around the room looking for Julia and Lucy, but was sidetracked by the principal announcing her arrival. The very people she thought she would never have to see again, swarmed around her. She smiled through clenched teeth as two specific teachers hugged her effusively, as if they had never had the staff meeting arguments and snarky remarks when she had won County Teacher of the Year.

She finally spotted Lucy and Julia and stomped over to them. Before she could open her mouth, though, Lucy handed her a glass of wine and said, "We tried. Honestly. But they wanted to do this and we couldn't stop them."

Kate took a deep breath and then a deep gulp of wine. "I guess I believe you."

"Look, it's your favorite restaurant and they're all paying, so eat up and drink up and try to be merry. It can't be that bad listening to a bunch of people tell you how wonderful you are." Julia laughed and kissed Kate on the cheek.

Kate smiled and finished her wine. "Okay, where's the rest of this bottle?" The three walked arm in arm to the table that was set up as a bar and stayed close to that corner of the room. She was grateful that Julia and Lucy distracted many of the "well-wishers" while Kate tried to make the best of it. She had to admit that Julia was right about the accolades boosting her ego. And then one of the young student teachers plugged his iPhone into the restaurant's speaker system and Kate could let the wine remove her inhibitions. She started to sway to the music.

It was close to midnight when she pulled into her driveway. She had limited herself to two glasses of wine and had carefully adhered to the speed limit. But she was tired. The boxes containing twenty-five years of teaching and now occupying the trunk and back seat of her car, would have to wait until morning. Crosby, the tabby she had found on her doorstep a couple of years ago, greeted her when she opened the front door. She was never sure if his dog-like behavior was because he was happy to see her, or because he was hungry and his meowing was annoyance about her staying out so late. Whatever his reason, she liked to be welcomed when she opened the door.

She had to admit that she was surprised by the generosity of her coworkers. Not only had they paid for her retirement dinner, but they had also chipped in on a five hundred dollar Visa gift card. She was a difficult person to buy for and she was pretty sure Julia and Lucy had done some heavy duty convincing. She recalled some of the gifts others had gotten like expensive jewelry or sets of luggage and was glad that she didn't have to feign appreciation at what she would have considered to be hugely impractical and probably ugly. Or worse, a weekend at some beauty spa where she would have had to endure facials and mud baths and manicures. That just wasn't her cup of tea.

She picked up Crosby and flopped onto the couch. "Well, kiddo, here we are." He purred as she petted him. "First day of the rest of our life. I wonder where this next chapter will lead." She closed her eyes and started to nod off, but then jumped up and startled the cat into running under the coffee table. "I've got to go to bed. Too much wine and too much cake."

She picked up the purse she had left on the couch and took out her phone. She noticed she had a voicemail and listened to it as she walked toward the bedroom. She stopped short in the middle of the hallway and gasped. She stumbled into the bedroom and sat down on the bed to listen to the message again. She looked at the clock; she'll have to wait til the morning to call.

She finished her pre-bedtime routine in record time, even curtailing her usually meticulous flossing. After climbing into bed, she tried to read but couldn't keep her mind on the story and read the same sentences over and over. She shut the book and turned out the light, but she knew that sleep would elude her. That was one strange voicemail. She lay flat on her back staring at the ceiling and waited for the sun to come up.

2

THE SUN WAS BLINDING AT THAT
TIME OF THE MORNING. She had tried to
leave after nine so she'd miss the rush hour
traffic crossing the Golden Gate Bridge, but
there didn't seem to be any time of day or night
when traffic wasn't heavy around San Francisco.
MapQuest said it should take forty-five minutes
to get into the city but it never seemed to take
less than an hour. She kept moving the visor to
block the sun and between that and looking for
the weather report on KCBS, she kept her mind
off the disconcerting mission that lay ahead of
her.

The phone call last night had been
unnerving. She didn't know this guy, Peter, but
his news had jolted her back to a time in her life
she had worked hard to forget. And now she
would be visiting the apartment of the man who
had broken her heart; the only man she had
ever loved enough to marry.

She had met Martin in college. Most of the Sixties icons had either died from drug overdoses or were barely living in the aftermath. The hippie movement was still alive and kicking, though, but it was less about drugs, sex and rock and roll, and more about politics and the environment. In fact, it was at a political rally that their eyes met and drew them together. They became inseparable within days, moved in together within weeks, and married within months.

They say opposites attract and their backgrounds were worlds apart. Kate was from New York City. She had gone to private school and was raised by her father who was a high school English teacher and ultimately a best-selling author. Her mother died shortly after she was born. Martin came from Mississippi and had never known his father. His mother had been a blues singer and much of his childhood had been spent on his grandparents' farm. But the attraction was strong and deep, and although they lived in a liberal enclave at a time when much was overlooked, the fact that Kate and Martin were an interracial couple was still an anomaly.

The bridge traffic wasn't as bad as she had expected, and before she knew it, she was headed south on Divisadero Street. Martin's apartment was in The Castro, a San Francisco district that became one of the first gay neighborhoods in America. In the early part of the twentieth century it was a working class neighborhood of Scandinavians and then the Irish. In the forties, during World War II, thousands of gay servicemen were dishonorably discharged. They gravitated to San Francisco and landed in The Castro. That was the beginning of what would soon be a steady influx of gays.

After 1967 and the Summer of Love, just on the other side of Buena Vista Park in Haight-Ashbury, the flight of working class and middle class families into the suburbs intensified. They say that Herb Caen, the famous writer for the San Francisco Chronicle, instigated a mass invasion when he wrote in 1970 that every gay in San Francisco should take a cab to the corner of Castro and Market one Friday at eleven in the morning and take over the Twin Peaks Tavern. In 1977 Harvey Milk, who owned Castro Camera, became the first openly gay San Francisco Supervisor and that cemented The Castro as a gay oasis. Twin Peaks Tavern is still going strong as a gay bar.

Kate arrived at Martin's apartment and to her surprise, found a parking space just a few houses down the street. It wasn't until she got out of the car and read the sign that said Permit Parking only that she understood why she found a space so easily. She turned her hazard lights on and hoped for the best. She certainly didn't expect to stay long. She would just pick up her box and leave. She was actually a little spooked by being in Martin's apartment, especially since he wouldn't even be there.

It wasn't a large apartment building, four stories with two apartments on each floor, she guessed. It was one of those stripped down Victorians: once beautiful and ornate, but now rather nondescript. She saw the buzzer for Martin's apartment and pushed it. No one answered her ring for a couple of minutes. Just as she was about to press it again, the front door to the building opened and an attractive, muscular fiftyish man stood smiling in front of her. He wore tight jeans and a white T-shirt with a red awareness ribbon and the words SAN FRANCISCO AIDS FOUNDATION written across his chest. He reached out his hand and said, "You must be Kate. I'm Peter. We spoke on the phone."

Kate shook his hand tentatively, a little taken aback by the words on his shirt. "Yes. Hi. Is that how Martin died?" She nodded toward his chest.

"Yes. He'd been HIV positive for years, but hadn't contracted full-blown AIDS until three years ago, just after his longtime partner died. It was almost as if Martin waited so that he could take care of John first."

Kate smiled. "That doesn't surprise me."

"He was an exceptional man and an extraordinary friend. Come on up. I couldn't remember where the buzzer was inside the apartment to ring you in." She followed him up the stairs to the third floor. The door to the apartment was ajar, and as Peter pushed it open, she could see an elderly black woman sitting on a chair in the living room. Kate stopped short and gasped when she saw the woman. "Ruby, Kate's here," Peter said as he walked into the room.

Ruby sat stiff and motionless, staring out the window. She didn't move her gaze or speak, but nodded ever so slightly in response. Kate wasn't sure how to respond and decided not to acknowledge the nod or Peter's comment. She just walked into the room, glancing around guardedly. The apartment was small and its furnishings were sparse but stylish. It was a far cry from their hippie days with bookshelves made from cement blocks and planks, and a mattress on the floor. She was curious to know what Martin had ended up doing career-wise, but once she saw that Ruby was there, she just wanted to exit as quickly as possible. Anyway, her car was illegally parked and the last thing she needed was a ticket or a tow. "Where's the box?"

"Oh, it's in the bedroom. Let me get it for you."

"I'll come with you," Kate added quickly and followed Peter into the bedroom. There were piles of boxes, all neatly stacked and labeled. The only pieces of furniture were a bed and a dresser. Peter lifted a box off a pile with "KATE" written in neat block letters.

"You did all this packing of his stuff?" she asked.

"Oh no. Martin did all this the last couple of months until he couldn't stand for any length of time. The apartment looked pretty much like this the last few weeks. The only difference was Martin was lying in the bed."

Kate smiled again, remembering what a neat freak he had been. "So he had boxes for all the people in his life?"

"No. Most of the stuff is going to thrift stores. There are just a couple of other boxes going to specific people."

Kate cleared her throat. "What about Ruby? Won't she take anything?"

Peter sighed. "Martin and Ruby were estranged after he came out. They hadn't spoken in thirty years. I called her when he was dying, and they were able to have a phone conversation before he passed away. She just arrived yesterday by bus from Mississippi."

"So she didn't see him before he died?"

"Nope."

"Then why did she come?"

"To get the few things he had left her and maybe to assuage some guilt. Anyway, Martin had sent her a ticket before he died."

"Too bad she didn't get here in time, I suppose," Kate said, but she didn't sound particularly sorry about it.

Peter smiled. "I can see there's no love lost between you and Ruby."

"You got that right. She and Martin fought terribly when he married me, you know. I guess being gay is even worse than marrying a honky! She probably thinks it was my fault. Like I was the reason he became homosexual."

Peter put his arm around Kate's shoulders. "I think it's very sad, though, that a mother and son don't speak for their whole adult lives."

Kate looked into Peter's eyes and thought of her own relationship with her father. Her mother had died when she was a baby and it had obviously left a huge hole in her heart that her father's love had never been able to fill. She took a deep breath and let it out with a barely audible sigh. "Yes. I suppose it is." She bent down and lifted the box.

"Let me help you bring it to your car."

"No. I'm fine. It's not too heavy. I can manage it." She walked back in the living room. This time Ruby looked into her eyes. Kate decided to take the high road. "Nice seeing you again, Ruby." No matter how much she tried to soften her voice and color it with sweetness, the words sounded extremely sarcastic.

Ruby's answer was an icy stare. Peter opened the door to let Kate out. "I'll go down with you. Is your car parked nearby?"

"Yes, just a few houses down." Peter and Kate left.

"Thanks for coming, Kate." Peter opened the downstairs door. "Martin spoke about you a lot in his final days."

Kate stiffened. "We had a powerful bond."

"How long were you married?"

"Not long. A few years."

"That long before he came out?"

"That long before I knew. You're a good friend, Peter, to take care of all this for him."

"Martin did this for many of his friends." He shrugged. "It's what we do."

Kate nodded and went to her car, hoping there would not be a ticket on the windshield. To her relief, there was none. She put the box in the trunk and got into the driver's seat. She turned off the hazard lights but didn't want to leave just yet. The day had been stressful enough, but seeing Ruby had brought it to the next level of anxiety. She sat pensively for several minutes, wondering if a visit to a museum or a good restaurant in the city would help. She decided she would rather just go home and open this box. It was so weird that he would have anything of hers still, all these lifetimes later.

3

KATE PULLED INTO HER DRIVEWAY AND TOOK THE BOX OUT OF THE TRUNK. Crosby greeted her at the front door. He was definitely an unusual cat. "Hey Crosby, let's go see what's inside." She put the box down in the middle of the Oriental rug that covered the polished, hardwood living room floor. The box was taped securely. She wondered if it had been packed for forty years, or whether Martin had just found the items recently. And whatever could they be? Maybe he had some of her old records or tapes. Maybe even some of her clothes—isn't it about time for those peasant blouses and long skirts to be back in vogue? There might be some books or pictures of the two of them. She took a pair of scissors out of the kitchen drawer but when she got back to the living room, she found herself unable, or unwilling, to open the box.

She went to the bathroom and made herself a cup of tea, anything to avoid the task at hand. But then she realized that she didn't have to open the box. Martin would never know and no one else would care. Was she afraid to revisit that time in her life? They were mostly happy memories. It was just the breaking up that had been hard.

She paced around the house, and then put on some old classic rock and roll music to enhance the mood. As she expected, the music was motivating and she finally cut the tape. Lying across the top was an old bandana, the one that had always been hanging around Otis's neck. Otis had been her dog when she met Martin but the two had become inseparable so when she and Martin split up, she had let him take the dog. When she lifted the bandana out of the box, his ID tag fell out. There were some pictures of the three of them in various places. Kate had her own copies but she hadn't looked at them for a lot of years. She didn't enjoy bringing up old memories, and it certainly wasn't pleasant to be looking at how young they had once been.

She and Martin were both eighteen and bright-eyed, curious, eager college freshman embracing their independence. They were many miles from home, and home for both of them had not been of the white picket fence/Ozzie and Harriet variety. The relationship between Kate and her father had always been warm and loving, but they had both looked forward to the freedom they would be given on the day she went off to college. Martin and Ruby hadn't been close even in his childhood and his grandparents had been the ones who actually raised him. They were the ones who had instilled in him his thirst for knowledge and urged him to leave their farm in Mississippi to go away to college. It certainly wasn't affection or acceptance that Kate and Martin were searching for; they had both always felt loved. It was more a search for a sense of belonging to kindred souls.

She shuffled through the pictures fairly quickly. She was starting to dislike the emotions that were welling up. But she did stop at one particular image. She didn't have a copy of this one. They were at the beach. She was sitting on the bench of a picnic table with Otis sitting at her feet and Martin on top of the table, playing the guitar. How ironic that just as she looked at this photo, Janis Joplin's voice resonated through the room. "Freedom's just another word for nothing left to lose." But Kate refused to get caught up in that spiritual web of cosmic connections and coincidences.

She put the pile of pictures aside and glanced through the rest of the items. There were some record albums, books, and cassette tapes, all with her name in black magic marker. She must have forgotten them when she'd moved out. But then there was a pile of letters: love letters from the beginning of the relationship, angry letters when they were fighting, and newsy ones when she was away for a few days visiting her father. But then there were the ones filled with despair and anguish when they had broken up. Martin had arranged them in chronological order, neatly tied together with a ribbon. She opened the first one and started reading.

They wrote often for the first month or two. He had tried hard to explain that it wasn't her. He was young and naive and had hoped that somehow she could change him. She just wrote from her heart at how she had been hurt and angry, upset that he had lied to her. But he convinced her that he had not lied; it was that he hadn't accepted his own homosexuality. He had tried to turn off his attraction to men; he had truly loved her and wanted the marriage to work.

The last one she read, the last one she had written that he had never answered, was the hardest for her to read. He had been her husband and she had loved him. She knew that she had probably never stopped loving him. But she had finally understood and resigned herself to the fact that their marriage was over. She wished him well and asked him not to contact her again. She would send him the divorce papers to sign and he could mail them back, but not to write her or call her. And he hadn't.

She wiped the tears that had dampened her cheeks and put everything back in the box. Then she carried it into the spare bedroom that was more like a storage room/office/studio. It was where she kept the boxes she rarely opened, a desk with her computer, a keyboard and an easel. The art supplies were there in preparation for a retirement that she hoped would reawaken her creative side. Her phone rang just as she found a spot in the closet under some plastic tubs filled with teaching materials.

By the time she got to the living room and got the phone out of her purse, it had stopped ringing. She saw the missed call and recognized the number as Peter's. She waited for the voice mail; assuming that he had found something else that was hers. She decided that she wasn't curious anymore and didn't need to add to the crap she was trying to get rid of anyway. Her plan was to leave very little behind when she started her Peace Corps stint. She would start fresh when she returned. She went to her list of missed calls and pressed his number. "Hi Peter. It's Kate. No, I didn't listen to your message."

"I'm sorry, Kate, but I didn't know who else to call."

"What's up?" she asked.

"Ruby collapsed. I called 911 and they brought her to San Francisco General."

"What does the doctor say?" Kate asked.

"She had a heart attack. He said he's not surprised considering everything that she's been through. She is eighty-five."

"I don't understand what you want me to do. She must have family you can call."

"Yours is the only number I had."

"But I'm not family."

"More than I am."

"Hardly," she said sarcastically.

"Do you know any relatives I can call?"

"Martin never talked about his relatives, other than his grandparents who would be dead by now, of course."

"I don't know what to do. I have to finish cleaning out Martin's apartment by tomorrow or another month's rent will be due."

Kate looked at the clock and sighed. She felt sorry for Peter. It wasn't his responsibility anymore than it was hers. He had certainly done more than his share in helping Martin. "I guess I can come, but it'll be a while until I can get there."

"When do you think you'll be here so I can tell the hospital?"

"I don't know. More than an hour for sure."

"Thanks, Kate. Call me when you get to the hospital. Ciao."

Kate hung up the phone and flopped onto the sofa. She wasn't sure if she was angrier about having to drive back down to the city or at having to see Ruby again. It isn't easy to put on a sweet disposition toward someone who treated you like shit. The worst part was that she had always wanted to know Ruby better. After all, she was Martin's mother and she had led an interesting life as a blues singer, traveling around the South playing in rural honkytonk roadhouses and urban ghetto dives.

She decided she should probably eat something before she left for the hospital. She went in the kitchen and filled Crosby's bowl before opening the refrigerator to find it as empty as usual. She shopped as she did when she lived in New York when she picked up groceries every day. No one drove so you bought only what you could carry.

She managed to find some rice cakes and an apple and threw them in a bag to eat in the car as she drove. She wanted to get the whole unpleasant task over with as quickly as possible. Then she could get home to her first day of retirement.

4

KATE HAD ALWAYS TRIED TO PLAN HER TRIPS INTO THE CITY SO AS NOT TO COINCIDE WITH RUSH HOUR. Now it was dusk, aggravating her already unpleasant mood. It took her two hours to get to the hospital after all, exactly what she had told Peter and what she had thought she was going to avoid by eating in the car.

She parked the car, took a deep breath and wished she had not given up on meditation and yoga. This would have been a perfect time to chant "Om" to release the tension that was causing her teeth to clench and her shoulders to stiffen. But she had given up on it after just a few sessions. She had found jogging worked faster for de-stressing. She took a couple of laps around the parking lot so by the time she got to the emergency room, she was even able to feign a smile.

"I'm here for Ruby Thomas."

The clerk looked at her quizzically. "How are you related?"

"I'm not, exactly."

"Huh?"

"I was her daughter-in-law . . . once."

The clerk looked at the receptionist who shrugged her shoulders and went back to her phone call. "I guess that's close enough." She handed Kate a clipboard. "Fill this out please. The man who came in with her couldn't."

Kate glanced down at the papers. "Well, I can't answer these questions either."

"You were her daughter-in-law."

"I haven't seen the woman in thirty years. How would I know about her health or her insurance? I don't even know where she lives."

The clerk took the clipboard back with a sigh. "Wait here. I'll get the doctor."

Kate went back to the waiting room and joined the crowd of stone-faced people hacking, sneezing, bleeding, whimpering and sleeping. She searched for a seat as far away from the coughers and sneezers as possible. She always forgot to bring a book in these situations and wound up playing Solitaire on her phone. She had gotten through three games before the clerk called her up to the window.

"The doctor will speak to you now." The clerk pointed to some double doors. It had been many years since Kate had been inside an emergency room. In fact, her expectations were based more on watching the television show *ER*, than on her own experiences.

"So you are Ruby's daughter-in-law?" The man who spoke to her didn't look much older than her high school students.

"Uh, no. Or yes. I don't know. I guess you can call me that if you want."

The doctor gave her an inquisitive look and shrugged. "Okay. Whatever. Anyway, Ruby is quite sick. She had a heart attack and is stable now, but we need to monitor her for at least twenty-four hours before we can release her. Does she have a history of heart problems?"

"I have no idea. I haven't seen her in thirty years."

"Apparently she was supposed to leave tomorrow morning on a bus to Mississippi, but she is not in any condition to do that."

"Is she awake? Does she know what's going on?"

"Barely, but she's adamant that she doesn't want to stay in the hospital."

"So keep her here. Make her stay."

"I can't, legally. If she wants to leave the hospital, she can just walk out."

"She's an eighty-five year old woman who you just said was barely awake. How is she going to walk out of here?"

"You'd be surprised what people can will themselves to do. And then they collapse a few blocks away and make themselves worse or they die."

Kate had to smile as she shook her head. It was just like Ruby to be stubborn and defiant. "Well what do you want me to do?" she finally said.

"Perhaps you can talk her into remaining here for at least a couple of days."

"You've got to be kidding," Kate laughed. "If anything, I should probably tell her to leave. Then maybe she'd stay just to go against me."

"Well, she definitely can't ride on a bus for two or three days."

"Well if she can't go home and she won't stay here, what's the alternative?" Kate asked. It didn't take long for Kate to understand the Doctor's silence and raised eyebrows. "Oh, no. No. You don't understand. She hates me."

"You're family, aren't you?"

"Not now. And I never was in her eyes."

The doctor's pager went off. "Excuse me, I have to answer this. I'll talk to you later. She's in there." He pointed to a room and rushed off.

Kate looked at the door. She considered running out and letting the hospital deal with the whole situation. Didn't they have resources for this kind of thing? Then she thought of Peter and all he had done, which, in turn, reminded her that he had asked her to call him when she got to the hospital. She would call him and maybe he'd have an idea, and it also gave her a little more time before she had to confront Ruby.

She pressed his number on her recent call list. She made a mental note that it would probably be a good idea to put him in her contacts. "Hello, Peter. It's Kate. We have a problem."

"What happened? Is Ruby okay?" Peter asked.

"I think so. The doctor said she's stable, but she needs to be monitored and she refuses to stay in the hospital. And of course, she can't ride on a bus for three days or however long it takes to get to Mississippi."

"How can she refuse? Can't they make her stay?"

"Apparently not."

"I've gotten rid of the bed here and anyway, I'm bringing the keys to the landlord tomorrow morning."

"I guess I could put her up in a hotel," Kate mused.

"She probably needs to have someone with her."

Kate sighed. "I suppose so."

"What are you going to do?" Peter asked.

"Why is everyone asking me what I'm going to do? Since when did I become the—"

Peter stepped in with a calm voice. "I know this is weird and extremely uncomfortable and probably a million other things, but I have a small studio apartment—"

"I didn't mean that you should take her in," Kate interrupted. "I'll try to talk to her." She laughed. "Maybe I can make her see that her alternative is worse than staying in the hospital."

"Good thinking, Kate," he laughed with her. "That might just do the trick."

"I'll keep you posted." Kate hung up and walked back to Ruby's room, this time with a bit of resolve and determination in her step.

She pushed open the door to Ruby's room slowly and was relieved when she saw her in bed with her eyes closed. She tiptoed in and saw that Ruby was hooked up to a couple of machines and had an IV coming out of the top of her hand. What could she do if the doctors and nurses refused to unhook her? Would she take them out herself and run away? That's absurd. Of course the doctor could make her stay, maybe not legally, but he could figure out a surreptitious way to do it.

She looked around the room for a chair but didn't see one. She went out to the nurse's station. They were scurrying around as a couple of EMTs pushed a gurney through the double doors with what was obviously a critical patient. Kate decided she didn't really need to sit down and went back into Ruby's room. She leaned against the wall and watched Ruby sleep. Before she knew it, she had slid down to the floor, closing her own eyes. She had finally relaxed, feeling sure that there was no way Ruby could leave and she was therefore off the hook.

A nurse came in to check the machines and woke both Ruby and Kate. "Wake up Ruby. It's time to take your temperature." Kate stood up quickly and moved to the bottom of the bed.

Ruby opened her eyes and mouth just enough for the nurse to insert the thermometer. But then she saw Kate and she opened her eyes and mouth so wide that the thermometer fell out. "Peter called me," Kate said quickly. She didn't want Ruby to think she was there by her own volition.

The nurse chattered incessantly about how young Ruby looked for eighty-five while she waited to get the temperature reading. She removed it, read it, and charted it. "I'll get you a chair."

"That's okay. I don't need one. I won't be staying long."

"Suit yourself." The nurse left abruptly.

"They needed a next of kin and apparently I was the best they could come up with." Kate tried hard not to sound sarcastic. Ruby didn't answer so Kate continued. "Is there a relative I can call?"

"No." Ruby finally spoke.

"How about a good friend?"

"No."

Kate sighed loudly. She didn't attempt to hide her annoyance. "The doctor said you need to stay so they can run some tests on your heart. Have you had heart problems?"

Ruby ignored the question. "I want to go home."

"You can't. The doctor doesn't want to release you yet."

"I don't care what he wants!" Ruby started to get out of bed, pulling on wires and tubes.

"Ruby!" Kate reached over to one of the machines that had started to move. An alarm went off, and a nurse rushed in and turned off the alarm.

"You have to stay in bed Ruby," the nurse said as she gently pushed her back.

"Please. I want to go home."

"I'll get the doctor."

Kate came around to the side of the bed and watched a tear roll down Ruby's cheek. It was then that she realized how awful this must be for Ruby. She was about to say something but was glad that the doctor came in before she did. It would be better coming from him.

"Ruby, you can't take out the catheters," the doctor admonished.

"I'm okay now. I don't want to stay here."

"You really need to stay for at least a couple of days so we can monitor you and run some tests."

"I said no. Now please take these tubes out of me."

"You are not in any condition to get on a bus by yourself and ride for three days."

"Is there any other alternative to staying in the hospital?" Kate asked.

The doctor took a minute to answer. He turned away from Ruby and looked into Kate's eyes. "If she stayed with you and you brought her in every day to be checked."

Kate looked at Ruby who turned her eyes toward the wall. She took that to mean it would be okay with her and looked back at the doctor. "Do I have to bring her here or can I find a doctor or hospital near where I live in Sonoma County?"

"I can recommend a heart specialist up there."

"How long would I have to stay?" Ruby interjected. She took the words right out of Kate's mouth.

"That's hard to say right now. The doctor monitoring her would have a better idea in a couple of days."

"Don't you have some idea?" Kate asked. "A week?"

"Probably two at the very least."

Ruby and Kate finally looked at each other. Neither cracked a smile, but both their facial expressions showed apprehensive resignation.

"We need to get the discharge papers ready. It will be about an hour." The doctor and nurse left.

Kate glanced at Ruby who had her eyes closed. "Did Peter bring your stuff here or is it still at Martin's apartment?"

Ruby opened her eyes and looked at the closet. She still didn't speak. Kate went to the closet and took out a small, battered, leather suitcase. Ruby had probably had this antique since the 1940's and it might even be worth some money on EBay. Kate took the dress off the hangar and opened the suitcase to get out some underwear. "Stop!" Ruby screamed.

"I'll get the nurse to help you get dressed."

"I don't need a nurse. Just let me be to get dressed by myself."

"You need the nurse to unhook all these machines." Ruby sighed. "I'll see if I can find one." Kate went to the nurse's station and found the nurse sitting at the desk, filling out some papers. "Are those Ruby's discharge papers?"

"No, but I'll do them next."

"She needs to get dressed, but she's still hooked up to the machines and the IV."

The nurse turned to the clerk. "Get one of the med students in there. They can do it." The clerk got up and went into another room.

"Thanks," Kate said sarcastically. The nurse did not look up. Kate went back into Ruby's room. "A med student will be here to unhook you and help you get dressed."

"I said I don't need help getting dressed!"

"Fine!" Kate left. She dialed Peter's number and spoke to his voicemail. "I'm taking Ruby home with me, much to her dismay." She laughed. "And mine too, I guess. I'll let you know how it's going." She hung up and closed her eyes. This was not going to be easy, but two weeks wasn't too bad. Then she thought about the nuts and bolts. She didn't even have a bed in her spare room. And it was a mess.

She got up and went to the coffee machine. She was tired enough to drink anything that even resembled coffee. It was brown and said coffee on the button she pushed, but that was about the only way they were related. She stood against the wall sipping the disgusting liquid, watching the sad, scared, weary faces of the patients.

She finished her cup of brown liquid that somewhat resembled coffee. She hesitated before going into Ruby's room. She figured she had been gone long enough, but she certainly didn't want to walk in on her. She headed to the nurse's station to find the nurse who was supposed to do the discharge papers, but everyone was scurrying around and she was nowhere in sight. Kate went back to Ruby's door and knocked. "Are you dressed?" There was no answer. She knocked again and raised her voice. "Ruby? Ruby!" Still there was no answer. She opened the door gingerly. Ruby was sitting upright on the bed with the open suitcase next to her, but still wearing her hospital gown. Kate walked in and watched Ruby brush some tears off her face with a tissue. "I can help or get a nurse. Which would you rather?"

"Get a nurse."

Kate left silently and went back to the nurse's station. This time she took matters into her own hands and interrupted the commotion. "Someone needs to help Ruby Thomas now. No med student has shown up."

"Okay. It'll be just a minute," the clerk answered.

Kate waited a few minutes and then got more assertive when she noticed a couple of people standing around laughing. "Would you please help Ruby get dressed so she can leave?" One of the nurses gave her a piercing look and headed toward Ruby's room. Kate waited outside until the nurse came out. "And where are her discharge papers?"

"I'll try to find out." The nurse disappeared.

Kate walked in and saw Ruby standing at the sink, washing her face. "Do you need help getting back to the bed?"

"No."

"I've asked for the discharge papers."

"Okay."

Ruby shuffled back slowly, but she made it by herself. She sat down and they both looked down at the floor. Finally, the door opened and both the nurse and doctor walked in.

"Here are the papers," the nurse said.

"I want you to understand that you are leaving against my wishes." He held out a piece of paper. "You have to sign this AMA. It stands for 'Against Medical Advice,' so if anything happens, you cannot sue the hospital or me."

Ruby snatched the paper out of his hand. "Just give me a pen. I'm not going to sue you!"

Kate suppressed a smile. She decided to take Ruby's lead and took the folder out of the nurse's hand. "If we have any questions about it, we'll let you know. I imagine most of it is common sense." The nurse looked at the doctor and shrugged while Kate read through the papers. "I'll call if we have any questions. I'll get my car and pull it up to the entrance." Kate left before the nurse or doctor could respond and this time, it was Ruby who suppressed a smile.

5

THE CAR RIDE WAS MOSTLY SILENT, INTERRUPTED ONLY ONCE BY KATE AS THEY APPROACHED THE GOLDEN GATE BRIDGE. "Do you want to listen to the radio?" she had asked.

"I don't care," was Ruby's response. Kate decided to leave it off. Best not to give Ruby any more ammunition to inflame the situation. She would probably hate Kate's choice of music. And Ruby would probably scoff if she turned on NPR. Since conversation was definitely not in the cards, the only sound was the whirr of the tires and the wind whistling through the windows.

They reached Kate's house in less than an hour. Thank heaven for that. Kate pulled up in front and got out. She started to walk up to the house, but then went back to open the car door for Ruby. Ruby had kept her suitcase on her lap throughout the ride so she had no choice but to hand it to Kate. Kate took the suitcase and offered her hand to Ruby, but she wouldn't take it. She held onto the doorframe instead to lift herself up. Kate shook her head and shut the car door. She would let Ruby hobble up the walk by herself. But she kept the suitcase.

She didn't look behind her until she had unlocked the front door, and that's when she saw that Ruby had stopped halfway up the walk. She was breathing hard and holding her chest. Kate walked back, and this time Ruby took her arm.

When they got inside the house, Crosby greeted them as always. "You didn't tell me you had a cat," Ruby said.

"Are you allergic?"

"No. You just didn't tell me." Crosby had already started rubbing against Ruby's leg.

Kate wasn't sure what Ruby had meant. Perhaps Ruby just didn't like cats, so she picked him up. "Do you want to sit in the living room for a bit while I remake the bed?" Kate asked.

"Where am I sleeping?"

"In my bedroom. I'll sleep out here on the couch."

"I can sleep on the couch."

Kate looked at Ruby hard. It was time to get real. "No Ruby. You can't. You need to sleep in my room. I'll bring your suitcase in there now. Why don't you sit out here for a few minutes while I get the room ready." And with that, Kate took the suitcase and the cat into the bedroom. She glanced into the spare room as she walked past and grimaced thinking of what it would take to make it into a second bedroom. But the thought of spending at least two weeks sleeping on the couch was even less appealing.

She went back to the living room and was about to ask Ruby if she wanted something to eat, but her eyes were closed. She had fallen asleep sitting in the chair. Kate returned to the spare room to start the arduous chore of cleaning it up, but then remembered the discharge papers had said to get some prescriptions filled and to call the doctor for an immediate appointment.

She also needed to go to the grocery store. Besides the fact that there were was a food list of very specific foods that Ruby shouldn't eat, Kate knew that Ruby would never eat the food that Kate bought. Ruby had probably never seen the inside of a natural foods store. She sighed. Once again the reality of the situation hit her. Well, she would call the doctor's office for an appointment and get the bed made for Ruby before starting to clean out the spare bedroom. She would wait for Ruby to wake up before going out for the food and prescriptions.

After she finished making the bed, she walked back into the spare room and looked around. Where to begin? This was not how she wanted to spend her day. She piled up some boxes and stuck them in a corner. The easel could be folded up and returned to the closet where it had sat for years before planning for a retirement that was apparently going to be postponed. She moved the computer, desk and printer into her bedroom and went to the kitchen to get the cleaning supplies.

When she walked into the kitchen she glanced at the phone and remembered about making the doctor's appointment. She tiptoed into the living room to get her purse. She didn't want to wake up Ruby because she enjoyed not having to make conversation. She wondered if she and Ruby would spend the whole time pretending to be nice to each other or have a major blowup.

She got the number and made the phone call. Apparently, the doctor at the hospital had already alerted the doctor's office that Ruby would be calling and had impressed the urgency on them. They were quite accommodating, and she was able to make the appointment for first thing tomorrow morning.

Ruby slept for a couple of hours, and by the time she woke up, the spare room was crowded but clean. There was just enough room for a twin sized air mattress that Kate would buy when she went to pick up the prescriptions. Obviously, Ruby would still need to sleep in

Kate's bedroom, but now, at least, there would be a door to shut.

"Are you hungry?" Kate asked when she saw that Ruby's eyes were open.

"No."

"You need to eat to get your strength up." Kate racked her brain trying to think of what she had that Ruby would like. "How about some eggs and toast?"

"Just a soft boiled egg."

Kate went to the kitchen and cooked the egg. "Do you want some tea?" she called from the kitchen.

"Coffee," Ruby answered.

Kate entered the living room with a piece of paper in her hand. "The information sheet from the hospital says you're not supposed to drink coffee. Caffeine isn't good for your heart."

"I don't care what the paper says."

Kate stared at her silently and pursed her lips. "How do you like it?"

"Black."

Kate went back into the kitchen. When she returned to the living room with the egg and coffee, she noticed that Crosby was comfortably purring on Ruby's lap. She set the plate and cup on the table next to the chair and sat on the couch with a pad and pen. "Tell me what you like to eat. I'll go to the grocery store when I go out to get your prescriptions filled."

"I don't care. Anything you buy is fine."

"Ruby, please. Tell me what to get. You won't like what I eat."

"How do you know what I like?" Ruby snapped back.

Kate couldn't answer that one. Ruby was right. She hadn't seen this woman in more than thirty years, and she didn't even know her well then. How could she know what Ruby liked? "You're right," she finally said. "But I would like to buy you what you want."

"Whatever you get is fine."

"Do you want anything else at the drugstore besides your medications?"

"No."

Kate sighed. "Okay, then. Do you need anything before I go? Shall I show you where the bedroom and bathroom are?"

"I'll find them."

Kate watched as Ruby continued petting Crosby and didn't touch her egg or coffee. "I'll see you in about an hour."

"Take your time."

Kate wasn't sure if Ruby meant that sarcastically. "I will." Kate hurried out before Ruby could answer back.

Ruby was not in the living room when Kate returned. Her egg had not been eaten, but the coffee cup was empty. Kate put the groceries away before looking for Ruby to give her the medicine. She brought a glass of water with her. She found Ruby asleep in the bed, her clothes on the chair. Apparently, Crosby had a new best friend because he was curled up next to her. "Ruby?" she shook her shoulder gently. "You need to take a couple of pills. You're supposed to take them every four hours."

Ruby opened her eyes. "I don't want to take them. I don't like the way they make me feel."

"But you have to take them, at least today. We see the doctor tomorrow morning and you can talk to him about it." Ruby sighed and took the pills and glass. "Was there something wrong with the egg?"

"Stop worrying about my eating habits."

"Well, I think you should eat to help you get better. And I just wondered if maybe you like your egg cooked differently."

"It has nothing to do with how you cooked it. I'm just not hungry. I'll eat when I'm ready."

"Fine!" Kate left the room. She waited until she got to the hall to roll her eyes.

Kate spent the rest of the day getting the spare room more livable: blowing up the air mattress, hanging up her clothes in what room she could find in the closet, cleaning the bathroom. Ruby slept most of the day, or pretended to. When it was dinnertime, Kate debated about whether or not to ask Ruby what she wanted to eat, or even whether she wanted to eat at all. She decided to make herself a big salad and just ask Ruby if she wanted some.

She tapped lightly on the bedroom door before entering. "I'm making myself a salad. Do you want some?"

"Do you have any soup?"

"I could make some butternut squash soup pretty quickly."

Ruby scrunched up her face. "Squash soup? Never heard of it."

"It's delicious. It will be ready in about half an hour." Kate left before Ruby could change her mind. She was surprisingly excited to actually be doing something for Ruby. What was that about! She was just pouring the soup into a bowl when Ruby hobbled into the kitchen. "Oh, I could have brought it to you."

"I can walk, you know." Ruby sat down at the kitchen table and Kate brought her the bowl. "Do you have some more coffee?"

"Should you have coffee at this late hour?"

Ruby gave her a sardonic look. "I've been sleeping all day. Does it really matter?"

Kate laughed. "No, I guess not." She started the coffee maker and sat down with a bowl of soup as well.

"Where's your salad?"

"I decided to have soup too."

"You don't have to on my account."

"I'm not. I like it."

They ate in silence. Kate wanted to ask Ruby if she liked it, but didn't. She must have, though, because she finished her bowl. Or maybe she was just starving since she hadn't eaten all day. She waited to see if Ruby would actually give her a compliment. Ruby didn't say a word.

Kate brought her the coffee and took the empty bowl. "Would you like some more?"

"No thank you."

"Do you want to watch television?"

"No." Ruby got up with difficulty and started walking toward the bedroom with her coffee mug. The coffee spilled over the side as Ruby tried to keep it steady.

Kate took the cup from her. "I'll carry it." Ruby didn't object. Ruby got into bed as Kate put the cup on the night table. "Do you want anything else?"

"No."

"You should take your medicine again." Kate handed her the pills. Ruby swallowed them, washing them down with the coffee. "Do you want me to wake you to take the next dosage?"

"No. But would you hand me my knitting bag?"

Kate got a carpetbag that must have been even older than the suitcase. She hadn't noticed it before and wondered where it had come from. Maybe it had been hidden at the bottom of the suitcase. She handed it to Ruby. "I've always wanted to knit."

"You don't know how?"

"No."

"Didn't your mama ever teach you?"

"She died when I was a baby."

Ruby didn't speak for a moment while she took her knitting out of the bag. Finally she said, "Oh."

Kate decided to give up hoping for anything but scorn from Ruby. Maybe if she could just lower her expectations, she wouldn't have to continue to react and be disappointed. So she didn't answer or roll her eyes, and she didn't shake her head, but she couldn't keep a quiet sigh from escaping. "Goodnight Ruby. Call me if you need anything." She picked up Crosby who seemed startled. He had grown to like this new arrangement of sleeping positions and partners. But Kate was damned if she was going to let Ruby win this competition over the cat's allegiance. As soon as she got back to the living room and sat down with Crosby on her lap, however, he jumped off and scurried back into the bedroom. Kate could hear Ruby's doting voice as she petted him.

6

KATE SLEPT FITFULLY, WISHING SHE HAD SPLURGED AND BOUGHT THE MORE EXPENSIVE AIR MATTRESS. But she was trying to get rid of stuff, not accumulate more. She couldn't just attribute her insomnia to that, though. She was worried about Ruby. Did she take her medicine? Was she in pain? She hated that she cared so much. Maybe it was just that she didn't want her to die in her house. She looked at her phone and saw it was five-thirty. That was a reasonable hour to get up.

She put her head inside the door to the bedroom and saw Ruby fast asleep with Crosby curled up at her feet. She refused to let the tinge of jealousy take over. Why shouldn't an old sick lady get some comfort from a cat? She went to the kitchen to make coffee. The doctor's appointment was at nine, so she had plenty of time to do whatever she would have done this morning if this whole Ruby incident hadn't happened. Yet, she hadn't really planned to do anything. That had been the point of the first few days of her retirement. So there she sat, waiting for the proverbial pot to boil so she could pour herself a cup of coffee. She would have checked her email if she hadn't stupidly moved the computer into the bedroom where Ruby slept. She took her cup of coffee into the living room and sat quietly on the sofa, contemplating how she was going to get through the next two weeks.

Things started stirring about seven-thirty. Crosby came out looking for breakfast. Kate could hear the water running in the bathroom so she knew Ruby was up. She waited to see if Ruby would come out asking for coffee or something to eat, but she didn't. She just went back to bed so Kate poured a cup of coffee and went in after her. "Do you want something to eat with your coffee?" Kate asked, setting the cup down on the night table.

"Maybe a piece of toast."

"Butter? Jam?"

"Both."

"How did you sleep?"

"I slept."

"Did you take your medicine?"

Ruby glared at her and answered irritably, "Yes!"

Kate took that response as a signal that their relationship had not improved overnight and left to make the toast. She waited until she got to the kitchen before muttering to herself and slamming drawers.

The doctor's appointment was uneventful in that nothing much was established. Ruby was reluctant to answer any questions with anything but a yes/no, and the only question she had for the doctor was when could she go home. She didn't talk about her dislike of the medicine's side effects. She didn't give much of her medical history. She was unresponsive to the doctor's questions about her pain level. At least she allowed him to do more tests since he was quite adamant that he couldn't give her a definitive answer on when she could leave until he had that information back from the lab.

Kate, however, asked a few questions of her own. She wanted to understand what to expect and how much caretaking or nursing she would have to do. But he wasn't much help other than to say that she would have to play it by ear. He said his nurse would call after the results came back from the lab and then they could schedule the next appointment.

They drove back to Kate's house in silence, both of them disappointed that more hadn't been settled. This doctor had merely confirmed what the hospital doctor had said about a minimum of two weeks. Kate asked Ruby again if there was anything special she wanted from the grocery store. They could stop on their way home and once again, Ruby was noncommittal.

They were home by eleven, and Ruby went straight back to bed. Kate had already decided not to cancel her dinner plans with Lucy and Julia. They had wanted to take her to dinner to celebrate her retirement. She had also decided to try to get past the discomfort of someone else living in her house and live as normally as she could.

She tried to sort through some of the boxes of teaching materials. She was definitely going to get rid of those. She had wanted to find a new teacher just starting out who would love to not spend his or her paltry salary on these items. But she realized that the easiest thing might be to donate them to the thrift store and take the deduction. Her heart wasn't in it, though, so she gave up quickly. She wanted to go online, but Ruby never left the bedroom. Maybe this was the time to buy a laptop, but she hesitated. One doesn't buy new things when they are trying to shed thirty years of stuff.

Ruby finally got out of bed about three in the afternoon and came into the kitchen looking for something to eat. She claimed that she wasn't hungry but knew she needed to eat. Kate offered to make her something, but Ruby took a banana out of the bowl and sat at the table. "Is there any more coffee left," she asked.

"I'll make a new pot," Kate rushed to do it before Ruby had a chance to protest. But Ruby didn't even try. She wasn't the kind of person to respond with compassion and concern about troubling anyone, at least not Kate. "Do you mind if I use my computer?"

"What? Why are you asking me? Why should I care?" Ruby replied.

"Well I didn't want to disturb you since it's in the bedroom."

"Use it whenever you want. It's your house."

Damn right it is, Kate said to herself. The annoyance she felt at being inconvenienced was evolving into anger at being told what to do. But she would continue to take the high road. "Let me know when you want to go back to bed." And with that she turned abruptly and went to her bedroom.

Ruby must have found something to do in the living room because before Kate knew it, an hour had passed. She had answered some emails and gotten lost in a search for heart attack information and side effects of the medicines Ruby was on. Kate wanted to know what to expect and how long the recuperation period was since the doctor had been less than helpful. Of course, Ruby's lack of responsiveness hadn't given him much to work with.

Kate shut down the computer and went to find Ruby to tell her she could have the room back. She figured Ruby had fallen asleep on the sofa or something, but when she checked the living room, it was empty. She went to the kitchen and saw Ruby leaning on the counter, looking out the window at the back yard. The dishes had been done and the counter was wiped clean. "Thanks for doing the dishes," Kate said.

"This is the most pitiful back yard I've ever seen."

"I know. I had always meant to plant a garden. I just never got around to it. I didn't have the time. It's on my retirement to-do list."

Ruby shook her head and walked slowly out of the kitchen. Kate followed after a few minutes and found that Ruby had gone back to the bedroom and Crosby had joined her on the bed.

Her exasperation had turned to downright rage. This woman could still get to her. The whole situation would be laughable if it wasn't so damn infuriating. Here she was, opening her house to someone who had shunned and scorned her as well as her own son. Not only did she open her house, but was at her beck and call. And she treated her like shit.

"I'm going out to dinner with some friends. Do you want me to make you something to eat before I go?"

"No."

Kate let out an exasperated sigh and went to the bathroom to get ready. "I'm leaving now," Kate called from the living room. "I'll be home in a couple of hours." She left abruptly, not waiting for the response that probably wasn't going to come anyway.

7

THE WAITER APPROACHED THE TABLE AND RAISED THE EMPTY BOTTLE OF WINE. "Another?" he asked.

Julia, Lucy and Kate smiled at each other and shrugged. "This is a celebration, after all," Lucy said.

"Sure. Let's do it," Julia nodded to the waiter.

"Do you want to see the dessert tray?"

"I think we will just have the wine for dessert," Julia answered. "And I'll take the check."

"No you won't," Kate said.

"As I said, this is a celebration. Julia and I are splitting it," Lucy answered.

"Really? A celebration? Of what?"

"Your retirement."

"Retirement? What retirement? You seem to have forgotten about my house guest."

"Is it that bad?" Julia asked.

"It's pretty bad."

"Is she demanding?"

"No, quite the opposite. She basically sleeps all the time and barely eats."

"Well, that's good, isn't it? She leaves you alone, then."

"Just her presence is enough to get my goat. You have no idea how badly she treated me when Martin and I were married!"

"I'm sure you're not the first daughter-in-law who was treated badly by her mother-in-law."

"But she didn't even know me. It would be one thing if she just didn't like me. But this was pure racism."

"What did she do that was so terrible?"

"I could have dealt with the silent treatment I always got, but the name-calling and lies . . ."

"Seriously? Name-calling?" Lucy asked.

"She wouldn't even try to hide it when I was in the same room."

"What kind of lies?" Julia asked.

"That I was a rich white girl from New York who couldn't be trusted. That we were all alike, marrying Black men as a rebellion against our parents and that we would leave them as soon as we found someone rich to marry us."

"But Martin didn't believe her so what does it matter?"

"It didn't matter for years, but now she's in my house! And I have to take care of her!"

"That's tough. I agree. Now you have to be nice to her instead of just forget."

"And besides that, I haven't shared my home with anyone since my father lived with me in Venice Beach and that wasn't a barrel of fun either."

"Well, it won't be for much longer." Lucy always tried to find the bright side. It was something Kate tried to emulate, not always with much success.

"So just ignore her. Give her a taste of her own medicine." Julia was the opposite. She had a hard time finding the bright side of anything. But she was damned if she was going to let anyone get the better of her. It wasn't a trait that Kate admired, but Julia sure was a lot of fun and a loyal friend.

The waiter brought the second bottle and thankfully the conversation took a different turn. Kate was a careful drinker and stopped the waiter from pouring too much into her glass. She let the other two finish the bottle while she sipped her glass slowly. When the bottle was empty, she looked at her watch. "Jesus! We've been here almost three hours!"

"Well, it was a delicious meal and great company!" Lucy gushed.

Kate kissed her on the cheek. "You're so lovable. But we should get going. The waiter is probably pissed that we've taken up his table this long."

"There you go, Kate, always worrying about everyone else," Julia smirked.

"Yeah, well, I suppose I could have worse faults."

"What's happening with the Peace Corps stuff?" Lucy interjected.

"I'm just waiting to hear my assignment. It should be any day now." Kate stood. "Are you ladies okay to drive? I had a lot less than you two and I'd be happy to take you home."

"We're fine. You're such a lightweight!"

"I don't think Kate's a lightweight. She just drinks less by design," Lucy added.

Kate ignored their attempts at humor. "Thanks for dinner. You really didn't have to pay for me."

"You know, soon you'll be living only on your pension."

Kate knew that Julia meant it as a joke, but it wasn't like it didn't cross her mind that things would be different for her financially now. "I'll know who to turn to when I'm living on the streets. See ya."

She went out to her car and sat in it for a minute before turning on the ignition. She didn't really want to go home, but Julia and Lucy were both tipsy enough not to filter their thoughts and conversation, and Kate was not in the mood for questions and advice. She didn't want to drive anywhere either. After all, she had been drinking, even if she had limited the amount.

When she arrived home, she unlocked the front door and found Crosby, meowing incessantly, just inside it. "What is it Crosby? Did you actually miss me?" Kate admitted to feeling a smug sense of relief. But rather than leap into her arms, Crosby ran down the hall toward the bedroom. "What's with you Crosby?" Kate followed him as he ran back and forth between Kate and the bedroom door. Ruby was lying unconscious on the floor next to the bed. "Ruby!" She knelt down, shaking her shoulders and calling her name. Ruby didn't wake up. Kate ran to the phone and dialed 911.

"I need an ambulance right away! My—"she paused for a split second —"mother-in-law is unconscious. She may have had a heart attack." She rattled off the address and ran back to Ruby's side. Crosby was already there, sniffing and meowing. Kate had taken CPR many years ago. She had needed it to renew her teaching credential. But she had never needed to use it and had probably forgotten everything she learned. She had watched the procedure done enough times on television shows, though, to have some idea of what to do. She decided to try. After all, it couldn't make it worse.

She opened Ruby's mouth and started blowing into it and to her surprise, everything she had learned came back to her. She didn't have to know whether her CPR attempt had worked or not, since the ambulance arrived immediately.

She ran to open the door and showed the EMTs into the bedroom where they quickly got to work. Kate picked up Crosby and stood in the hall. It wasn't more than a couple of minutes, and Ruby was on a stretcher. One of the EMTs asked her if she wanted to ride in the ambulance.

"I'll follow you to the hospital in my car. PVH?"

"Yeah. Go to the emergency entrance on McDowell." They left with Ruby while Kate stared after them, frozen, with Crosby in her arms. She finally put him down on the floor and gathered up her purse and jacket. She started out the door and then ran back to the living room to get a book to take along. It was already after ten, and she figured it would probably be a whole night of waiting.

8

KATE ARRIVED AT THE EMERGENCY ROOM HALF AN HOUR AFTER THE AMBULANCE. They wouldn't let her in to the examination area. Instead they took her to a clerk's desk to fill out pages and pages of paperwork. Of course, she couldn't really fill them out since she had no information to share about Ruby. She knew her name, age and that she was probably on Medicare but had no idea if she had a supplemental insurance policy. The administrative assistant was skeptical.

"Ruby was staying with you, correct?" the woman asked.

"Yes."

"And you don't have any idea where she lives?"

"I told you. Mississippi. But I don't know what town."

"What is your relationship to her?"

"Um . . . ex-daughter-in-law?"

"Is that a question? You don't know if you're her daughter-in-law?"

It was hard to decipher who was more annoyed with whom. They were both sarcastic and sighing with every sentence they uttered. "I was married to her son a long time ago and I didn't even know her then. Does that answer your question?"

"I suppose. Well, I'll need information from you, since you're the next of kin."

"I'm really not her next of kin."

"Oh for Pete's sake, just give me your name, address and phone."

Kate told her and signed her name. "She was in San Francisco General last week. Maybe they have more information. Why don't you call them?" And with that Kate darted out of the room.

She returned to the receptionist's window in the waiting room. "They're still working on her. Have a seat until the doctor or nurse comes out to get you." She wasn't much more congenial than the other woman. Kate sat down and opened her book, but barely finished a paragraph before her eyes closed.

"Miss McGee?" Kate opened her eyes and found that she was staring into the face of a man wearing green scrubs. She sat up abruptly when she realized she had been curled up on the bench. She glanced at the clock on the wall and saw that it read three o'clock. When she noticed only one other person in the waiting room, she figured it was a.m., not p.m.

"Yes?" she finally answered.

"You can come back and see Ruby now." Kate followed the man through the doors into a curtained off area. Ruby was lying on a gurney, hooked up to various tubes and machines. "She's sleeping, but the doctor will be in shortly to talk to you."

"Thanks," Kate replied. The man left, pulling the curtains shut behind him. She stared at Ruby who was snoring softly. A part of her felt sorry for this poor old woman who lay in a hospital two thousand miles from home. But a part of her also remembered how little this woman cared about her own son when he lay sick and dying. Not to mention how Ruby's narrow-minded intolerance had affected Kate and Martin's relationship, even if that relationship was doomed anyway. Luckily the doctor walked in before Kate could get too immersed in her past regrets.

"Are you the ex-daughter-in-law? I'm Dr. Green, ER attending." He reached out his hand to shake Kate's.

"Hi. Kate McGee." She nodded and shook his hand.

"Ruby is a very sick woman. If she were younger I'd suggest a bypass, but I'm not sure her body could handle it."

"So what are you going to do?"

"We'll admit her and have the heart specialist, Dr. Corning, take a look. Why don't you go home and get some rest yourself. Dr. Corning will call you after he's examined her."

Kate just stared at him without speaking. It dawned on her that her life of Riley was about to be turned upside down. This wasn't a temporary glitch in her plans, a couple of weeks taking care of an old lady who hated her. There would be lifestyle changes, thwarted plans, and hard choices.

"Ms. McGee?" The doctor tapped her shoulder.

"Uh, yes. Okay." Kate left quickly and drove home in a daze. At first, she followed her customary obsessing over how she would manage this new turn of events. But it was the middle of the night, and soon her mind turned to mush as she just tried to navigate her way home without falling asleep.

She stumbled through the door and picked up Crosby, thinking she would carry him to bed with her. But as soon as she got to her bedroom and saw Ruby's stuff, she was jolted back to reality. Instead of falling onto the bed, not caring that they were Ruby's sheets, or going to the air mattress in the other room, she put Crosby down and started rummaging through Ruby's suitcase. All she found were a couple of dresses, some underwear, and toiletries. Then Kate saw Ruby's purse and emptied it out on the bed. There wasn't much in there either: a comb, a handkerchief, a change purse with a clasp, and a bus ticket.

She took the ticket and went to the computer, but noticed the time. It was four a.m. Pacific Time. She wasn't sure what time zone Mississippi was in, Eastern or Central, but either way, this would have to wait. The Yazoo City Clerk's Office would not be open yet, so she would have to wait to see if they could help locate anyone. At that, she went back to the air mattress and flopped down, finally allowing her exhaustion to take over. Crosby did not follow. He fell asleep in the pile of Ruby's clothes.

9

KATE WOKE TO THE SOUND OF HER CELL PHONE RINGING. By the time she got her bearings and realized what room she was sleeping in and what room her phone was in, the ringing stopped and presumably went to voicemail. She glanced out the window and thought that it must be close to midday, since the sun was so bright. She didn't rush to get up and listen to the voicemail. She wasn't in any hurry to find out how much her life was about to be impacted. Crosby, however, was another story. He jumped on top of her and reminded her loudly that his breakfast was about four hours late.

"Okay, Crosby, I'll get up, but I have to pee first so you'll just have to wait another minute." It wasn't until after Crosby had been appeased and she had a full cup of coffee in her hand, that she listened to the voice mail.

"This is Dr. Corning's medical assistant at the hospital. Please come in as soon as possible so that the doctor can meet with you and Mrs. Thomas to discuss her condition."

Well, that didn't explain much. Kate decided to take a shower and finish what she had wanted to do on the computer before going to the hospital. She took her coffee into the bedroom and sat down at the desk. The Yazoo City, Mississippi city offices page came up on the screen. She found a phone number and dialed.

"Hello? I'm calling from California and I'm not sure what person or office I need to speak with. I'm trying to find the relatives of a woman who lives in your city." After being shuffled among several different people, she finally found someone willing to help: the city clerk.

"I'll see what I can do and call you if I find out anything."

"Please call me either way," Kate replied. "And it's kind of a matter of life and death. I mean, not mine, but Ruby's."

"I understand. I'll get right on it." Kate hung up with an ounce of relief and a pound of hope. The shower would help.

Before she left for the hospital, she made one more call. "Peter? It's Kate. Ruby had another heart attack and is in the hospital up here. I called the Yazoo City clerk and she is trying to locate some relatives because I really can't do this. Please call me when you get this message."

It was mid afternoon when she got to the hospital. Kate asked the clerk of the nursing unit to page Dr. Corning and then tiptoed into Ruby's room. She looked small and fragile in the bed, her eyes closed, hooked up to so many machines. No one was in the other bed and the room was barren: no personal effects, no cards, no flowers. Kate made a note to at least bring in her knitting bag. She stood by the bed and spoke quietly. "Ruby?"

There was a flutter of eyelids, but no response. Kate sighed and sat on the other bed to wait for the doctor. She didn't have to wait long, thank goodness.

"Good afternoon. I'm Dr. Corning." An attractive men bounded into the room. He had a dazzling smile, intense eyes, a kind voice, and a magnetic demeanor.

"Hi, I'm Kate," she smiled at him.

"Nice to meet you. So I understand that you're the ex-daughter-in-law? Sounds like there must be an interesting story there."

"Yes. Very interesting. And that would be ex for many years."

"I'd like to hear the story some time."

"Uh, sure." Was he flirting with her? It's always hard to tell with men that are so charismatic.

He picked up Ruby's hand and held it when he spoke. "Ruby? Are you awake? We need to talk." Ruby looked like a frightened rabbit when her eyes opened. They darted back and forth between Kate and Dr. Corning, but she didn't speak.

Kate decided to fill the void. "Ruby, isn't there anyone back in Mississippi I can call? A relative? A friend?"

"I don't need anyone."

"Yes, you do." Kate could not hide her exasperation.

Dr. Corning sensed the tension. "Let's all have a chat and see if we can come up with a plan." He sat down on the bed next to Kate. Good move, Kate thought. Let's all pretend to be one big happy family. She knew how much this conversation was going to be anxiety producing for both of them. Dr. Corning had no idea what he was in for. "Ruby needs bypass surgery immediately. Her arteries are blocked. Her age is a concern, though, for any major surgery." He glanced at Kate to see her reaction, realizing that Ruby would probably not have a discernable one.

"Are there any other options?" Kate asked. She wondered if her voice sounded too much like pleading.

"Angioplasty and stenting are possible options, but I'm afraid with Ruby having had two heart attacks, things are too far along to do anything else."

"What you're saying is that she needs bypass surgery, but she may not be able to tolerate it?"

Dr. Corning nodded. "Something like that."

"So it's risky to do it and it's risky not to do it? That doesn't sound like there are options."

"Maybe I should have said choice rather than option. Anyway, this is a decision you and Ruby will have to make together."

Ruby slammed her fist on the bed. "Why are you talking to her? This is my decision, not hers!"

Kate stood. "She's absolutely right! It is her decision. I have nothing to do with it." She walked out of the room, relieved, but also maybe a tad angry at Ruby's lack of gratitude. She went to the lobby and sat down, unsure what to do at this point. She didn't have to contemplate the situation very long.

Dr. Corning sat down next to her. "Ruby wants you to bring her things to the hospital."

"Is she going to have the surgery?"

"No. She refuses. But I need to tell you that she's a very sick woman. She will require help when she leaves the hospital."

"She doesn't want my help. She made that very clear."

"Then I'll have to ask the hospital's social worker to find some organization or agency to provide assistance."

"I think that's a great idea. I'll go home and get her things and bring them here tonight."

"I'll tell her you'll be back tonight."

Kate got up. "I've made a call to the city clerk's office in her hometown of Yazoo City, Mississippi. They are supposed to be looking for relatives or a friend. I'll let you know if they are successful."

"That would help a lot. Thanks, Kate." She started to walk away. "And by the way, I am still interested in the story behind you two."

Kate smiled at him. "It's a doozy."

Her cell phone rang just as she was getting into her car. She looked at the number and saw it was Peter. She decided to wait until she got home to give him the news. She didn't feel as desperate to talk to him now that she was out of the picture.

She called Peter back when she got home and informed him of Ruby's decision. Peter wasn't surprised. He had seen enough of Ruby to know she was a stubborn woman who relished her independence. And she certainly didn't want to be at the mercy of Kate of all people.

Kate waited until after dinner to bring Ruby's suitcase and purse to the hospital, hoping that maybe she would miss visiting hours so she could just leave them with someone in the lobby. She really didn't want to say goodbye to Ruby. But the lobby desk was empty, so she had no choice but to go to the unit clerk who was happy to let her go right into Ruby's room.

Ruby was awake. "I think I got everything. I put your knitting bag back inside the suitcase and your medicine bottles from the other hospital inside your purse. You should probably let the doctor know what you've been taking."

"I know that."

Kate shook her head. Ruby was a piece of work. Not an ounce of gratitude for all Kate had done. "Well, good. I'm glad you told them."

But just as Kate started to leave, the words finally came out of Ruby's mouth. "Thank you." They were barely above a whisper.

"You're welcome." Kate sighed before she left the room. She hadn't meant to sigh, and she didn't know if Ruby would understand what it meant. She wasn't sure herself whether the sigh was of relief or "it's about time."

10

KATE TURNED OVER, OPENED HER EYES, AND SMILED. She was in her own bed, the night table was empty of medicine bottles, and Crosby was asleep at her side. Her house and her days belonged only to her. She had big plans for this next stage of life and Ruby's intrusion had been more than a glitch. But now she could move on.

She went to the kitchen and started the coffee pot. There was a pile of mail on the table that she hadn't even had time to look through. She fed Crosby while waiting for the coffee pot to finish gurgling, poured a cup, and sat down to read the mail. Then the phone rang. "Please don't be the hospital telling me Ruby has changed her mind, " she muttered to Crosby. "Hello?"

"Kate? It's Julia. I got the name of that real estate agent from my sister."

"Oh good. Hold on a minute. Let me find something to write with." Kate rummaged through a drawer and found a pen. She took an envelope off the pile of letters. "Okay. I'm ready." She scribbled the name and phone number on the back of the envelope. "Thanks. I'll call her later this morning." She turned the envelope over and gasped. "Julia! I got the letter from the Peace Corps with my assignment."

"Well, open it! What does it say?"

Kate fumbled with the envelope and finally got it open. "South Africa! I'll be teaching at a girl's school."

"When do you go?"

"Not for a couple of months. It's a long process. Hey, I still want to take that trip to Hawaii. I can get the house ready to put on the market when we get back."

"I'm in! Find us one of those cheap last minute deals. Let's do Maui. I haven't been there in years."

"I'm on it." Kate hung up and took her cup back to the bedroom. She sipped her coffee and waited for the computer to boot up. She was calmer than she had been in weeks. "Maui here I come!"

After an hour or so of googling, and a couple of phone calls to Julia about dates and times, the travel plans were made. There were some pretty good deals on travel if you could leave with just a couple of days notice. A few more phone calls later and she had Jessica, her sixteen-year-old neighbor, feeding Crosby while she was gone, and Charlotte, the realtor, ready to meet with her when she got back. She hadn't heard back from the Yazoo City clerk, but it didn't matter anymore. She was too caught up in her travel plans.

Two days later Kate stood in the living room, her suitcase next to her on the floor, talking to Jessica. Crosby purred in the teenager's arms. "I can see Crosby is not too concerned about my leaving him."

"Hey, Crosby and I are good buds," Jessica answered.

"That does make leaving him a lot easier. So you have the key?" Jessica took it out of her pocket to show her. "Everything's on that pad on the kitchen table."

"We'll be fine. Have a good trip."

"Thanks. Don't spoil him too much." Kate took Crosby from Jessica. "Be a good kitty while I'm gone."

Julia came to the door. "You ready?"

"Yes ma'am!" She put Crosby on the floor and the three women left the house together.

11

RUBY SAT ON A CHAIR, STARING OUT THE LARGE FRONT WINDOW OF THE HOSPITAL ATRIUM. There were a handful of other patients in there, talking to each other or watching television. But Ruby sat alone. It was not as if the other patients hadn't tried to start up a conversation, but Ruby ignored them until they finally stopped trying. It had been more than a week since the doctor had given her the news of her heart condition. He had finally stopped trying to convince her to have the surgery.

Miss Barker, a nurse, approached with a small paper cup of pills and another small cup of water. "Here, Ruby. Dr. Corning says you can go home tomorrow."

Ruby took the pills and nodded.

"You'll have to sign an AMA Discharge, though, since you refuse to follow his advice." Then she added as an afterthought, "AMA stands for Against Medical Advice." Miss Barker made no effort to conceal her disdain.

"I know that." Ruby answered.

"You know what?"

"What AMA stands for."

"Okay. Then you'll sign it?"

"I'll sign it."

"Is someone coming to get you?"

"I'll take a bus."

"A bus? You can't take a bus."

"I'll manage."

"Where do you live?"

Ruby sighed loudly and pointedly. "Yazoo City."

Miss Barker looked confused. "Is that here in northern California?"

Ruby shot her a look that could have melted an iceberg. "Mississippi."

"You're going to take a bus all the way to Mississippi by yourself?"

"Yes," Ruby answered smugly. Miss Barker shook her head and left, returning momentarily with Dr. Corning.

"Ruby, you're in no condition to ride a bus all the way to Mississippi," Dr. Corning said.

"Thanks for your concern, but that is my plan."

"There's no bus to Mississippi from here. You'll have to get to San Francisco."

"Is there a bus to San Francisco?"

"Yes, but how are you going to get to the bus station here?"

"I imagine I'll take a city bus."

"The city bus that stops at the hospital won't take you to the Bus Terminal."

"Then I suppose I'll take a taxicab." Dr. Corning and Miss Barker glanced at each other and simultaneously shrugged their shoulders in surrender.

"Okay, Ruby. I'll get the AMA papers ready for you to sign. I'm going to have to ask the social worker to interview you." Dr. Corning turned to Miss Barker. "Anne, please see me in my office after rounds so that we can get the papers filled out."

"Why do I have to talk to a social worker?" Ruby asked.

"I have to document that you are mentally competent to make this decision. The social worker, Mrs. Ludlow, might also be able to help you prepare for your trip." Ruby sighed and scowled. "Shall I call Ms. McGee and let her know what you've decided?"

"No!" Ruby answered vehemently. Dr. Corning left to speak to another patient in the atrium.

"Are you ready to go back to your room, Ruby?" Miss Barker asked.

"Yes," Ruby sighed. She knew that Miss Barker would bring over a wheelchair. Ruby got in it, reluctantly. She had already tried to resist using one, but they had convinced her that it was hospital policy. Miss Barker pushed Ruby's wheelchair out the door and down the hall.

Mrs. Ludlow arrived shortly after lunch. Ruby answered her questions cryptically. "It sounds like you are fully aware of the consequences and are still determined to leave." Miss Ludlow was more neutral in her attitude than the doctor and nurse.

"Yes. I just want to go home."

"Will you see your doctor when you get there?"

"Yes." Ruby knew how to answer the questions appropriately.

"Would you like me to call the cab company and set up a time tomorrow to be picked up?"

"Yes. Thank you."

"The driver will want cash. Do you have it or do you need to cash a check?"

"I have it."

"Okay, then. And please be careful, Ruby. This will be a long, arduous journey so ask for help if you need it."

"I'll manage just fine."

Mrs. Ludlow left and Ruby took out her purse, hidden under the covers of the bed. She opened the change purse and counted her money. She thought she'd have enough for the taxi and the bus to San Francisco. Luckily she still had the bus ticket Peter had bought her. She hoped they would not give her a hard time about changing the ticket. A lot of time had passed since the original return date. She had her checkbook if it came to that.

The next morning was a flurry of activity for Ruby. Mrs. Ludlow had scheduled the taxi to come at nine. "Are you ready for your trip?" Mrs. Ludlow asked as she entered Ruby's room bright and early.

"I'm waiting for the nurse to come with the papers."

"Did you get help showering and getting dressed?"

"I showered myself. I needed a little help with the zipper."

"The bus for San Francisco leaves at ten. It shouldn't take more than a few minutes for the cab to get you to the bus station, so you'll have plenty of time."

"How long is the bus ride to San Francisco?"

"It takes about an hour. The bus to Yazoo City leaves at noon. That gives you plenty of time to get to the gate."

Ruby nodded. Dr. Corning had been right about one thing. Mrs. Ludlow had been very helpful. Miss Barker brought the AMA papers in to be signed at eight. Dr. Corning made one last appearance to witness the signing, just in case Ruby had come to her senses. But she was as adamant as ever.

Her bag was packed; she was fully dressed and sitting in her wheelchair by eight thirty. Her purse was on her lap, her suitcase and knitting bag on the floor beside her, as she waited for the orderly to take her to the front of the hospital. At eight fifty-five the orderly appeared along with Miss Barker. "Hand me my knitting bag, please," Ruby said. Miss Barker gave it to her and picked up Ruby's suitcase.

The taxicab was idling at the door when Ruby got there. The driver took the knitting bag from Ruby and the suitcase from Miss Barker and put them in the trunk as the orderly helped Ruby into the cab. It was a slow and laborious process, but she was finally inside. "Here are your discharge papers with information about your medications. Make sure you follow the directions and please see your doctor right away when you get home. We will send your chart and all the lab and test results. Take care." Ruby nodded but didn't say a word as the cab drove away.

The taxi pulled up to the bus terminal and the driver got out. He opened the trunk and took out the suitcase and knitting bag. He set them on the curb and opened the back door to help Ruby out of the cab. She took out her change purse and carefully counted out the fare plus a paltry tip. The cab driver frowned and got back into his cab. He drove away quickly, leaving Ruby standing on the sidewalk.

She leaned down to get her suitcase and knitting bag, then stood up slowly, wincing in pain. A young man on a bicycle careened illegally down the sidewalk. He had headphones on and was yelling into his phone, agitated and oblivious to his surroundings. He saw Ruby start to walk toward the bus depot entrance, but noticed her too late. He swerved to miss her but he clipped her arm and the edge of the suitcase and she fell face first into the concrete. He also fell, but got up quickly and picked up his bike. He rode away without stopping to see if she was okay.

Well, she wasn't okay. She was unconscious, her face bloody, and her knitting spread all over the sidewalk. A couple of people rushed out of their cars and a pedestrian pulled out his cell phone and called 911. One of the bystanders gathered the knitting and put it inside the bag.

A woman who had been walking out of the bus terminal rushed to Ruby and turned her over gently. She cradled Ruby's head in her lap, trying to wake her up. Another woman reached inside her purse and took out a handkerchief and a bottle of water. She dabbed some water on the handkerchief and handed it silently to the woman on the ground. She started gently wiping the blood off Ruby's face.

The ambulance arrived within a few minutes and the EMTs took over. Ruby went back to the place she had just left a few minutes earlier.

12

IT WAS WAY PAST MIDNIGHT WHEN JULIA'S CAR PULLED UP IN FRONT OF KATE'S HOUSE. "Thanks for driving to and from the airport. I'll put a call in to Charlotte tomorrow morning and have her come out to the house."

"Charlotte?" Julia asked.

"That realtor your sister used."

"Oh right. Senior moment, I guess."

"Or just utter exhaustion from a whirlwind trip to Maui."

"Well, I still don't think we needed to do every single activity just because it was recommended by the concierge."

Kate laughed. "I just needed to prove to myself that I still could."

"That's your issue, not mine. I know I'm getting too old for this."

Kate gave Julia a hug and opened the door. "Talk to you in a couple of days." She got her suitcase out of the trunk and fumbled for her key. That's the trouble with arriving back from a trip at night when you live alone, no one to turn the light on. She opened the front door and Crosby jumped off the couch to greet her. She picked him up. "Hey big fella. Did you miss me? You're looking fat and healthy. Jessica took good care of you. I'm exhausted. Let's go to bed." She carried Crosby in one hand and pulled her suitcase with the other, as she walked down the hall to her bedroom.

Crosby got her up earlier than she had wanted the next morning. But he was a cat, after all, and cats are not known for their altruistic, self-sacrificing nature. He was hungry and that's all that mattered to him.

She noticed the light flashing on the answering machine when she got to the kitchen to make coffee. Most of her friends used her cell phone to get in touch, but she still gave out her landline number to businesses or those she didn't know well. She played back the messages while she waited for the coffee to brew. The first one was from Charlotte, the realtor, asking her to call as soon as she got back so they could set up an appointment. There were a couple of sales pitch calls for solar energy and life insurance and a robocall asking for a donation to the Democratic Party. But then there was one from the hospital, asking her to please call Dr. Corning as soon as she got the message. It was a few days old, so she assumed that they were informing her about Ruby's discharge.

Needless to say, she didn't call anyone back except for Charlotte.

She made the appointment with Charlotte for later that afternoon and brought her cup of coffee into the spare bedroom. It had become a bit of a junk room since Ruby left. It still had the air mattress set up although it had lost most of its air. Martin's box was still sitting in the corner. She wanted to go through it but she needed to make the room neat and tidy for the real estate agent. It wasn't easy, though, to put things away without looking at them and reminiscing, so it took most of the morning to get the room looking presentable. She showered and cleaned the rest of the house and had just put a load of laundry in when the doorbell rang.

"What a perfect location! And a lovely house!" Charlotte bounded into the house with the predictable exuberance and confidence of a salesperson. She extended her hand. "So great to finally meet you. I'm sure you're tired from your trip. This won't take long." And before Kate had a chance to get any words out or even to open her mouth to respond, Charlotte was down the hall, peeking into rooms and taking notes. Kate took steps to follow her when Charlotte breezed past to the kitchen. "Don't let me interrupt you. I'll just look around and go back to my office to check comparables and then I'll be able to determine a listing price."

At that moment the phone rang so Kate didn't follow as Charlotte opened the back door to assess the yard. "Hello? Dr. Corning! Yes. I got your message, but I've been traveling. I just got back last night." She frowned and collapsed into a chair with a despairing sigh. "Oh no, what happened?" Crosby jumped onto her lap. "Okay. Bye." She put the phone down on the table. "Oh, Crosby!"

After a few minutes of sighing and scowling, she got up and went to the door. "I won't be much longer," Charlotte called up to her.

"There's not much to look at out there. I never got around to landscaping it."

"It would be a good idea if you could at least plant some flowers. It would definitely add to the appeal."

"It's on my to-do list."

Charlotte came back inside. "I'll call you later today with my recommendation. When did you want to list it?"

"Soon."

"Good. I'll get the papers written up as well and maybe we can get together tomorrow."

"Okay. Thanks." Charlotte was out the door as quickly as she arrived. Kate couldn't say she liked Charlotte or would choose her as a friend, but she certainly was businesslike and brusque: qualities you want in a realtor. Now to find out

the next episode of the Ruby saga that just
won't quit.

13

KATE ARRIVED AT DR. CORNING'S OFFICE ABOUT AN HOUR LATER. He was at his desk doing paperwork so she went right in and flopped into a chair across the desk from him. "So what happened to Ruby?" Kate asked, unsuccessfully hiding the irritation in her voice.

"She was hit by a bicycle in front of the bus station."

"What? You've got to be kidding!"

"She was adamant about going home and took a cab to the bus station. I did not release her so she signed an Against Medical Advice form."

Kate shook her head incredulously. "Can she walk?"

"Not very well. She broke some ribs and has a lot of bruising."

"She must be in a lot of pain."

"Yes and extremely weak. It's remarkable that she didn't break a hip or a leg. She has an amazingly strong constitution. There's nothing we can do for broken ribs. She just needs to rest and be on pain medication and they should heal. Medicare won't pay to keep her in the hospital because she doesn't need medical care anymore."

"Will Medicare pay for a rehab place?"

"No. They'd only pay for rehab if she had the bypass surgery."

"I don't see her changing her mind on that." Kate looked down at her lap and sighed.

"I don't either." Dr. Corning cleared his throat and smiled. "She asked for you."

Kate looked up at him, stunned. "She did?"

"She finally seems to understand her predicament."

They were silent for a few minutes. The doctor waited for Kate to speak first. She finally stood up and exhaled. "Let's go see Ruby."

They didn't speak as they walked through the hospital corridors. Dr. Corning was wise enough to see that Kate needed to digest this latest news. When they entered the room, Ruby was facing the wall. He touched her arm and said quietly, "Ruby? Kate's here." Ruby turned and looked at Kate with a quivering lip and tears in her eyes. "I'll set up your discharge for tomorrow." He left them alone.

"I need to go home and get the spare room ready for you. I'll be back tomorrow to pick you up." Kate reached out to touch Ruby's hand, but then took back her arm and just smiled. Ruby nodded and turned back toward the wall.

Kate took out her cell phone as she walked to her car in the hospital parking lot. "Jess? Hi, it's Kate. Thanks so much for taking care of Crosby. Is your Dad home? Thanks. Mike? Hi, do you still have that bedroom furniture in your garage? I need to borrow it for my spare room."

"I thought you were turning that spare room into an art studio or something more presentable than a junk room," Mike said.

"That was the original plan, so it would look nicer for a buyer."

"But?" Mike asked.

"I'm getting an unexpected guest," Kate sighed. "And I don't know how long she'll be staying. I need to clear out the room first, so give me a couple of hours. Thanks." This time she was not going to give up her bedroom. She hung up and drove home a little faster than she should, but she was a bit agitated, to say the least.

She cleared out the room as quickly as possible, piling things up in the garage. It didn't take long since she had just neatened it up that morning for Charlotte's visit. She called Mike and went to the kitchen. She saw the blinking light on the answering machine and pressed the button. "Hi Kate. It's Charlotte. Give me a call so we can set up an appointment tomorrow."

Oh great. Now what was she going to do? She couldn't have people traipsing in and out with Ruby stuck in the bed. Once again that woman has disrupted her life!

The doorbell rang and that got her out of her self-pitying attitude. Mike stood at the door with Jess, holding a mattress between them. "Thanks so much. This really helps me out." Mike and Jess glanced at each other. They both wanted to ask who the guest was, but figured it would be up to Kate to tell them. They shouldn't pry. But Kate never said another word about it.

They finished moving the furniture in and Kate promised to take them out to dinner to thank them properly. She enjoyed watching the interaction between Mike and Jess. Like Kate, Jess' mother had died when she was too young to remember her. Mike and Jess had the same easy-going, playful relationship she had with her own father. She missed him. At least right now she did. There had been many trying moments when they lived together in Venice. But they were both adults then and both of them had been set in their ways. It was not the same as it was when she was growing up in New York. She made a mental note to give Finn a call. It had been way too long. She took a look around the new guest room. The furniture was a little childish. It had been in Jess's room until she had begged Mike to let her redecorate it in typical teenage fashion. There was a twin bed, a night table and a dresser: serviceable and comfortable. Ruby would be fine.

Now Kate had to decide how she was going to handle putting the house on the market. She had planned to put it off a little while anyway to get the backyard looking better. She'd call Charlotte and use that as the excuse for waiting, telling her that she might be able to get more for it if the back yard was more landscaped. She went to the kitchen to call Charlotte back, actually feeling a little relieved that she could wait a while longer. She still hadn't been given a starting date from the Peace Corps, so she wasn't in a rush. She tried to be Lucy-like and look for the silver lining, but she found it hard to do.

14

KATE DIDN'T SLEEP TOO WELL THAT NIGHT. She tossed and turned, anxious about the days ahead with Ruby and what would happen to her Peace Corps plans. John Lennon was so right. Life happens when you're busy making other plans. She couldn't help but remember her father moving in with her when she lived in Venice. It hadn't been a medical emergency like Ruby; it was the death of his wife. That was hard enough, and she and her father usually got along pretty well — at least they did when he wasn't drinking.

But Ruby was an entirely different circumstance. Kate had never forgiven her for shunning her as a daughter-in-law just for being white. And then to find out Ruby had practically disowned Martin for being gay. Kate wondered how he would have felt about her taking Ruby into her home. But then she remembered how he had bought the bus ticket for Ruby when he knew he was dying. Martin was a good man and he had always treated Kate with respect, kindness, and affection.

She remembered the tears he shed when he told her that he couldn't reconcile the fact that he was gay, and that he had tried so hard with Kate. He loved her and wanted their relationship to work, but he couldn't deny who he was. He was truly devastated at how much he hurt her and he said he would never stop loving her, just not as a sexual partner.

It was Kate who broke off all ties. He had wanted to stay friends, but she couldn't handle it. She wondered if that had been a mistake. She had never had another long-term relationship after that. She traveled the world, moved to Venice, and had many short-term ones. By the time she moved back to northern California, she had pretty much left even those relationships behind. She wasn't celibate, but her liaisons were brief and superficial and they were becoming few and far between.

By the time she got to the hospital, Ruby was dressed and sitting in a wheelchair. The papers had been signed, and the frown on Ruby's face displayed her irritation at having to wait. Not a good beginning.

"Why don't you bring your car to the front entrance and we'll meet you there," the orderly told Kate. Kate nodded silently, afraid to open her mouth and annoy Ruby even more.

The ride to Kate's house was quiet; luckily it didn't take too long. When they got to the house, Kate helped Ruby out of the car and handed her the walker that the orderly had given them. Ruby hobbled up to the front door, and Kate carried her suitcase, purse, knitting bag, and cane. Crosby gave Ruby an exuberant, warm welcome, rubbing on her leg, and it was then that Kate felt like the icy atmosphere had finally started to thaw.

"I've fixed up the spare room for you," Kate said as she led the way. "I hope you'll be comfortable."

"I'm sure it will be fine." Kate put the cane, suitcase, purse and knitting bag down, unsure whether she should help Ruby into bed but afraid to ask. Ruby sensed the uneasiness. "I can manage now."

Kate breathed an audible sigh of relief. "I put a bell on the night table so you can ring if you need something."

"Thank you."

Kate hesitated before leaving. "Um, did you eat breakfast already?"

"No. That hospital food is awful."

"Would you like me to make you something? Eggs?"

"Just some toast and coffee."

"I'll get some water so you can take your pills."

"I don't want to take them. I don't like the way they make me feel."

"But they'll help with the pain."

"No."

"Okay, okay. I'll just get your toast and coffee." Kate picked up Crosby and left, knowing there was no point in arguing.

After Ruby ate breakfast she fell asleep and Kate called Charlotte. After explaining that she wanted to do some planting in the backyard before putting the house on the market, Charlotte made a pitch for a landscaping company that her cousin owned, but Kate was not interested. She'd lived with a barren, uncultivated yard and she would be damned if she was going to spend a bunch of money for some other person's enjoyment. The problem was that Kate had never embraced gardening as a hobby and in fact, was quite inept at it. But how hard could it be to plant a few flowers? Maybe the house would be sold before they started to look like crap.

She took her coffee to the backyard and looked around to get an idea of how much to buy. She'd need some tools, too. She shrugged. She'd just ask for help when she got to the store.

15

KATE WAS GONE FOR ABOUT TWO HOURS. After unloading the car and lugging the gardening tools into the backyard, Kate changed her clothes and peeked in on Ruby. Crosby lay curled up on the bed, both of them snoring contentedly. There was a part of Kate that wanted to smile at the picture, but mostly she felt jealous that her cat would warm up so quickly to Ruby again.

The man at the nursery had given her various implements, an assortment of flowers and plants, some bags of fertilizer and mulch. He also gave her advice that probably hadn't stuck with her, but she figured she could read the directions on the bags. And how hard could it be to dig a hole and put a plant in it? She started singing from "The Garden Song" by Peter, Paul and Mary. It had been a long time since the song had crept into her consciousness.

She dug for about half an hour. She had no idea when she was supposed to stop or how deep the holes should be. Well, she had the shovel, the rake and the hoe. She had no idea, though, whether or not the ground was fertile. But wasn't that why she had the bag of fertilizer? She stopped digging, threw some fertilizer into the holes and picked up one of the gallon pots that held pink roses. She stared at it, trying to figure out how to remove the plant from the pot. She pulled tentatively on the stem and leaves. "Ouch!" She'd forgotten about the thorns. She found a spot on the stem between the thorns and pulled again. It seemed to give slightly. She pulled a little harder and eventually the plant came out but most of the roots and soil were still left in the pot. She dumped the leftover soil and emptied the fertilizer into the hole and put in the plant.

Before she finished patting down the soil, she heard the loud, insistent ringing of a bell. At first she looked to her neighbor's yard to discover where it was coming from. Then she remembered that she had given Ruby a bell to ring if she needed something. The ringing was so forceful and relentless that she dropped the shovel and ran back to the house, afraid that Ruby had fallen again.

Kate rushed in the door and through the kitchen without glancing around and ran into Ruby's room. The bed was empty. "Ruby? Where are you?" Kate yelled as she ran toward the bathroom. When that room, too, was unoccupied, she ran back into the kitchen and found Ruby next to the window, leaning on her walker. "Are you okay?" Kate asked, slightly out of breath.

Ruby stared at her, shaking her head in disbelief. "I've been watching you. You don't know what you're doing out there."

"You could be a little more tactful." Kate said, laughing, although she was also a little irritated.

"You need help."

"How are you going to help me? You can barely move."

"I'll just tell you what you need to do."

"Okay, what?"

"Help me outside."

Kate took Ruby's arm with one hand, and together they walked slowly out to the yard. Kate grabbed a lounge chair and brought it to the area where she had been digging. She helped Ruby into the chair and stood with her hands on her hips, waiting for instructions. "So what am I doing wrong?"

"You killed that rose plant before you even put it in the ground!" Ruby snarled.

"What do you mean?" Kate asked.

"The way you got it out. You don't just pull a plant out of a pot! Didn't you notice the roots left in the dirt?"

"Well, yeah. But how do you get it out, then?"

"Get me that cane the hospital sent me home with."

Kate went inside and came back with the cane. "You're going to dig it out with your cane?"

Ruby shook her head in disgust and said, "Get another plant. Maybe that purple zinnia."

Kate looked over at the line up of pots. There were two different plants with purple flowers. "Which one is a zinnia?"

"Don't you know anything, girl? You ain't got the good sense God gave a rock!"

Kate sighed and went to the two pots. She pulled out the plant label stakes and found the one that said zinnia. She picked up the pot and placed it on the ground next to Ruby. "Here. Now what?"

"Lay the pot on its side."

Kate did that and looked back at Ruby. "Okay."

"Now hand me my cane."

"Huh?"

"Just do what I tell you."

Kate handed Ruby her cane and Ruby stood up and leaned heavily on her walker. She then lifted her foot and stepped gently down on the side of the pot. She used her cane to roll the pot and then stepped on it again. After that she tapped the bottom of the pot with her cane. "Why are you doing that?" Kate asked.

"Loosens the dirt. Now pull the plant out of the pot gently." Kate started to turn the pot right side up. "No! While it's on its side!"

Kate sighed and did what she was told. The zinnia came out easily, its roots intact and still in a mound of soil. "Ah. I see now."

"But you can't plant it here. There isn't enough sun. Go over to that hole you dug over there." Ruby pointed to the end of the row of holes Kate had dug. Kate took the plant and went to the hole. "What did you do to get the soil ready?" Ruby called out to her.

"I thought you just dig a hole and put the plant in."

"Don't you know anything?"

Kate's eyes blazed and she glared at Ruby. "I grew up in New York City! We didn't have a garden or a yard!" Ruby tried to get out of the chair, and Kate dropped the plant and rushed back to Ruby. "What are you doing? You can't get out of that chair by yourself!"

"I'm not an invalid." Ruby struggled and managed to get out of the chair, but Kate took her arm and helped her walk to the hole. "Give me a handful of that soil."

Kate took a clump of soil and put it in Ruby's outstretched hand. Ruby squeezed it into a ball. "What are you doing?" Kate asked.

"It's not friable. Too much clay. You need to add compost to break it up. Did you buy some?"

Kate went to her pile of nursery purchases and brought back a bag of mulch. "I thought I was supposed to put this on top after I planted."

"Yes, that's what mulch is for. But why didn't they sell you compost?"

"I don't know. I didn't ask for it."

"Oh dear Lord. I guess you can use mulch as compost, but you'll have to really mix it into the soil." Kate started to pour the mulch into the dirt. "Not like that! Let me do it."

"Why can't I do it?" Kate asked.

"Because you're doing it all wrong. Bring me that damn fool chair."

"What chair? The lounge chair?"

"No, that wheelchair they gave you at the hospital." Kate went inside and came back with a folded wheelchair. "Set it down right here." Kate opened it and placed it next to the hole. Ruby sunk into the chair slowly. She shook her head and mumbled, "You're as useful as a back pocket on a shirt."

"What did you say?"

"Nothing. Now open that bag of mulch and get me your garden tools. Set them all down here next to me and go about your business. I'll call you if I need you."

"No. I want to stay here and help." Kate brought the tools over. Ruby barked orders at Kate while Kate worked her tail off, digging and planting.

After a couple of hours, Kate helped Ruby inside. "I need a nap." Ruby grabbed her walker and started down the hall.

"Thanks," Kate called after her. Ruby just waved her hand as if to say "you're welcome" but didn't utter the words. Kate shook her head and smiled. She was starting to understand Ruby.

16

KATE SAT ON THE COUCH WATCHING TELEVISION AND PETTING CROSBY, CURLED UP IN HER LAP. Ruby had slept all through the afternoon and dinner. Kate felt terrible. She should have been adamant about doing the work herself, but Ruby had been insistent that it be done her way. And as far as Ruby was concerned, Kate was completely incompetent. Well, maybe Ruby was right, but Kate was a quick learner and as long as Ruby gave her instructions, she probably would have done just fine.

Ruby finally came into the living room, leaning heavily on the walker. Her knitting bag was draped over her arm. She put the bag on the floor and lowered herself slowly on to the sofa next to Kate. "Do you want some dinner? I can warm it up," Kate said.

"Maybe just a boiled egg."

"I made salad and pasta."

"Just an egg, please."

Kate shrugged and went to the kitchen to make the egg. Crosby scrambled onto Ruby's lap. Kate returned with the egg and a piece of toast. "I know you didn't ask for toast but I thought you might like some."

Kate expected Ruby to make a snide comment or one of her southern sayings, but instead she just said, "Thanks."

They watched television in silence as Ruby ate. When she was done, Kate took the plate into the kitchen and Ruby took out her knitting. Crosby was working on unraveling the ball of yarn when Kate returned. "You might want to keep that ball of yarn in the bag," Kate said as she sat back down.

"It's okay." Ruby replied.

They sat quietly for several minutes. Finally Kate said, "Maybe you could teach me to knit."

"I suppose so." Kate scooted right next to her as Ruby reached in her bag for another pair of knitting needles. "What color yarn?" Ruby asked.

"Anything's fine. Whatever you have most of."

"Just tell me what color."

Kate sighed. She could never do or say the right thing, even when she tried being accommodating and flexible. "Okay. I'll take green."

"I don't have green."

Kate's lips rose into a half-smile and she shook her head. "Okay. Blue." Ruby reached into her bag and took out a ball of green yarn and started to wrap the yarn around the needles. "But, that's green."

Ruby looked at it closely. "Hmm, so it is." Kate decided not to answer. Maybe Ruby's colorblind. Or maybe she doesn't see well or just didn't remember that she had green yarn. After all, she is in her eighties. "Now, watch how I do this. This is a knit and this is a purl stitch." Kate watched intently and after a few minutes she took the needles herself. She got her fingers stuck in the loops at first, but after a while she got the hang of it.

"This is fun," Kate said enthusiastically.

"No one ever taught you how to knit or garden as a child? That's a real shame."

Kate shrugged. "I lived with my father in a four room apartment in New York City."

"No granny? No auntie?"

Kate bit her lip to keep from blurting out something she'd regret. "No."

Ruby shook her head. "That must have been a sorry childhood you had."

Kate took a deep breath and put the needles down. "I had a wonderful childhood and a loving father who taught me many other things." She wanted to add that he had never abandoned her because he disapproved of the person she married, or who she had become. But she decided not to open up that can of worms. Dammit Ruby! Kate was just warming up to her and feeling sorry for her predicament.

Ruby must have sensed Kate's anger and maybe even realized that she ought to be on better behavior since she was pretty dependent on Kate. "Yes I'm sure he did."

Kate picked up the needles again, and they continued knitting together. Kate asked for help when she needed it. Crosby finally gave up playing with the yarn and fell asleep on the couch between them.

After a half hour or so Kate put the needles aside. "I have some Googling to do on my computer. Do you mind if I go in your room for a few minutes?"

"It's your house. You can go wherever you want."

"Well, I mean, were you planning on going to bed soon?"

"Good lord, girl. Didn't I just sleep all afternoon?"

"I guess you did." Kate got up and started to walk away.

"What'cha mean Googling?"

Kate smiled. "Google is a search engine. You can go to that site and find out just about anything you want to know."

"Never used a computer."

"Do you want to watch me?"

Ruby shrugged. "Okay." She put her own needles down and got up with difficulty. Kate held the walker steady, but Ruby pushed it away. "That thing is too bulky. Could you get me my cane?" Kate put the walker back and got the cane, and Ruby hobbled after her.

"You can sit here at the desk and I'll go get another chair." Kate helped Ruby into the office chair and turned on the computer. "It takes a minute to boot up," she said as she left the room. Ruby stared at the screen intently as the icons came up. She gingerly touched the mouse and moved it around, smiling as she watched the cursor move around the desktop. She inadvertently clicked on a folder and startled herself when it opened. She was laughing out loud when Kate entered with the chair. "What's funny?" Kate asked.

"I don't know what I did but all of a sudden this was on the screen."

Kate smiled as she set the chair down next to Ruby and sat in it. "You opened a folder. That's all. Do you want to set up an email account?"

"Huh?"

"Or would you rather learn how to use Google first?"

"Google!" Ruby laughed again.

"Does Google make you giggle?" Kate joined Ruby and pretty soon the giggling turned into full-blown laughter. They spent the next hour or so on the computer. Ruby was an eager student and also a fast learner.

17

IT WAS RAINING HEAVILY THE NEXT MORNING WHEN KATE GOT OUT OF BED. She started the coffee maker and went to Ruby's room to see if she was up. Crosby slept by Ruby's side and lifted his head when Kate peeked in. He stretched and began to knead on Ruby's stomach, rousing her. Kate crept away, afraid that Ruby would make some snide comment about waking her up. She went back to the kitchen and peered out the window at the torrential rains.

"Nasty weather today."

Kate looked up, startled. "Uh yes, it's unusual for this time of year."

"Too bad. I was hoping to do some more planting today."

"I guess it will have to wait."

"Guess so," Ruby answered.

"Do you want some breakfast?"

"Maybe some toast and coffee." Ruby hobbled to the kitchen table and sat down, while Kate poured the coffee and put the bread in the toaster. "Could you get my pills?"

Kate tried to hide her surprise. First, that she was going to take her pills, but mostly that she asked Kate to get them. It was probably the first time Ruby actually asked for help. "Sure."

Kate returned with the pills and placed them on the table along with a glass of water and the toast. "Thank you." Ruby smiled at her. Another first!

"Are you in a lot of pain? Maybe you worked a little too hard yesterday."

Ruby's smile turned to a scowl. "I'm not one to shy away from hard work."

"I didn't mean that. I know you . . . I was just . . ." Kate decided there was no point trying to explain to Ruby that maybe, just maybe, she was concerned about her. She changed the subject. "I have some errands to run. Do you need anything?"

"Nope."

"Okay." Kate no longer tried to cajole Ruby into asking for anything. She finished her coffee and left Ruby eating her breakfast and staring out the window.

Crosby came into the kitchen and meowed at Ruby. "Are you hungry, boy?" She started to call for Kate to feed him, but then stopped. "Let's find you something to eat." She got up slowly and shuffled to the cabinets. She opened a few doors and ultimately found some cans of cat food. "Here we are." She opened a couple more cabinets and found a plate, opened drawers until she found the silverware, pulled the tab, and scooped out the food. She bent down, wincing in pain, and set the plate on the floor. Crosby scurried over and ate heartily.

Kate entered. "Oh. I was just about to feed him." She glanced at Crosby and then back to Ruby. "Where did you find those cans?"

Ruby looked at her, guardedly. "In the cabinet."

"I didn't know I had any canned food. I feed him dry food unless he's in a picky mood." Ruby was quiet. Kate felt like a fool. Why did she have to say anything? Did it really matter in the big picture whether Crosby had canned food one day? "I'm sure you made his day. That's fine. Thank you for feeding him." Ruby nodded and left the room. Kate grabbed a couple of shopping bags and an umbrella and went out to her car.

When Kate got home a few hours later, the rain had diminished to a drizzle. She half expected to see Ruby in the back yard, digging and planting. As she put the groceries away, she peered out the kitchen window, but the yard was deserted. She checked the living room to see if Ruby was watching television and knitting, but that room was empty too. "She's probably napping," she thought. She tiptoed to

Ruby's room and peered in. Ruby was there, but not on her bed. She was sitting at the computer, hunting and pecking with painstaking effort and smiling. "It looks like you have the hang of it." Kate smiled too.

"I'm slower than molasses going uphill in January."

Kate laughed. "Do you want any help?"

"No. I can manage."

"Okay. Just holler if you get stuck. Can I make you some lunch?"

"Not hungry."

Kate shrugged and went back to the kitchen. After another hour or so, she realized that she would like to use her computer, but didn't want to upset the apple cart again. Things were going smoothly, and Ruby had finally relaxed somewhat. She decided to make some phone calls.

She called her father in New York, but he didn't answer. She tried Charlotte to update her, but she had to leave a message there too. Peter picked up his cell when she dialed and lent her a sympathetic ear. He apologized profusely for having gotten her life in an uproar by calling her to pick up the box. Kate assured him that he shouldn't feel badly and that, in fact, she was beginning to warm up to Ruby's quirkiness. After hanging up with him, she made plans for dinner with Julia and Lucy. Just as she got off the phone, Ruby walked in, using her cane, but with a decidedly livelier gait.

"Is there any more of that soup?" Ruby asked.

Kate got up and opened the refrigerator. "I think so. Sit down. I'll get it."

Ruby started to protest but stopped herself. She seemed to finally understand, like Kate, that a little effort into keeping the peace would pay off. "Thank you," Ruby replied as she sat at the table. Kate looked at her, and they smiled at each other. The smiles were almost genuine.

"I think I'll go on the computer while you're eating. That way you can take a nap this afternoon if you feel like it." Kate placed the soup bowl on the table as Crosby jumped onto Ruby's lap. "Now Crosby, you need to let Ruby eat her lunch."

"That's okay. He knows I spoil him and give him tastes when I eat."

Kate wanted to tell her not to do that, but caught herself. Instead she left and waited until she sat down at the computer to mutter to herself, "Who feeds soup to a cat?" Then she remembered the eclectic diet of Mother, the cat who belonged to her father's homeless friend Jed. Mother had become their cat when Jed became an elusive fugitive. Jed and Mother had subsisted on anything they could find to eat on the Venice Beach boardwalk. She smiled remembering those days when she and her father had somehow managed to live in the same house. Maybe learning to live with him had made it possible to live with Ruby now. He hadn't been that easy either.

After checking her email and doing a little Googling herself, she decided to give the room back to Ruby.

"The room's all yours," Kate said as she entered the kitchen. Crosby had just finished licking the bowl.

"I'll just wash my bowl."

"That's fine. I can do it. I was going to clean the kitchen anyway."

"Okay." Ruby stood slowly, wincing but trying not to show it. "I think I'll take a glass of water with me and take a pill."

"Are you sure you shouldn't lighten up on the digging and planting?"

"No!" she retorted defensively.

"I'm just concerned. I want you to help me. I really do." Ruby didn't answer, and Kate worried that all the mending of fences they had done was ruined. She watched Ruby take a glass of water and just before she was out of the room, Kate spoke. "I'm meeting friends for dinner tonight. Would you like to join us?"

Ruby stopped and took a minute to answer. "I don't think so."

"Well, it's not for a few hours. Think about it." Ruby nodded once and left.

Kate cleaned the kitchen, vacuumed the living room, and made a point to stay out of the back part of the house. She didn't want Ruby to feel like she was being watched constantly. But maybe she should show her how to turn on the computer in case she wanted to go back to it so she tiptoed to Ruby's room and found her back on the computer, intently typing and squinting at the screen. She looked up as Kate entered. "Do you need your computer?"

"No. I was going to show you how to turn it on, but apparently you figured it out."

Ruby scowled. "It wasn't hard."

"I didn't mean it like that. I'm sorry." Kate decided that the best alternative at this moment was to leave the room. As she exited Ruby called out, "What time are you meeting your friends for dinner?"

Kate turned around, thinking Ruby wanted to know when she'd have the house to herself. "Six-thirty."

Kate was about to say she would bring her something back from the restaurant when Ruby said, "I'll be ready."

Kate couldn't hide the shock on her face or the surprise out of her voice. "G-g-great," she stammered.

18

RUBY SAT AT THE KITCHEN TABLE IN HER BEST DRESS, HER HAT ON HER HEAD AND HER PURSE ON HER LAP. Kate entered wearing jeans and a sweater and said, "Oh it's not a fancy place."

"I don't go out looking like a farmer."

Kate smiled. "Well, you look very nice. We're going to a Japanese restaurant. I hope that's okay." Ruby shrugged and made a face but followed Kate out the door, leaning heavily on her cane.

They arrived at the restaurant and found that Julia and Lucy had already started on a bottle of sake. Kate realized she had forgotten to let them know that she was bringing Ruby. Oh well. Maybe that will change the topics of conversation, but Kate knew that they would be flexible and gracious. "You must be Ruby," Julia took her hand and helped her into the chair next to her. "I'm Julia."

"And I'm Lucy." Lucy waved to the waiter and motioned to bring another place setting. Meanwhile, Kate slunk into the other chair at the table, wondering why in the world she had ever invited Ruby to dinner and hoping she wouldn't say anything too offensive.

"I'm sorry. I forgot to let you know that Ruby was joining us," Kate said apologetically.

"It doesn't matter. I'm so glad to finally meet you, Ruby." Lucy, ever the diplomat! "Do you like Sake?"

"I don't know. What is it?"

"Try it and then you'll know," Julia said as the waiter approached with the place setting. "Bring another carafe of unfiltered Nigori and another cup," she told the waiter. She turned back to Ruby. "It's a wine made from rice."

"You probably won't like it," Kate chimed in. "Besides, your hospital discharge papers specify no alcohol."

Ruby glared at Kate and then turned back to Julia. "Wine made from rice? Hmm. Never heard of such a thing."

"Maybe you'd like to try some plum wine? That's also a Japanese alcoholic beverage but it's sweeter," said Lucy.

"I will try what you three are having." Kate sat back in her chair and kept her mouth shut. Let her mix the alcohol with the medicine. If Ruby wanted to kill herself, who was Kate to stop her! The waiter brought the sake and the extra cup. Lucy filled it and they all watched

Ruby take a sip and then make a face. "Maybe I'll have some of that sweet wine."

Kate flagged down the waiter and ordered the glass of plum wine. "Now, did you want to try sushi also? We usually get several different ones and share them."

Ruby furrowed her brow. "Sushi?"

"They're rolls wrapped in seaweed and rice. Often they're filled with raw fish but they can be filled with cooked fish, meat or vegetables too." Julia added. Ruby wrinkled her nose. "Or would you like tempura or teriyaki?"

"She shouldn't be eating fried foods," Kate quickly interjected. Ruby shot her a stern look. "Oh, eat what you want," Kate sighed.

"Tempura is shrimp and vegetables dipped in batter and then deep-fried." Lucy tried to diffuse the situation.

"Fried shrimp. I'll have that." Ruby sat back and took off her hat. The waiter arrived with Ruby's plum wine and Julia did all the ordering. Kate was thankful that her friends were exactly who they were. Lucy was always diplomatic and easy-going. Julia always took charge but not obnoxiously so. Kate was glad to let someone else make decisions, something she often tired of and sometimes had a hard time with.

After the waiter left and Ruby declared the plum wine to be delicious, they all relaxed and the conversation flowed comfortably and freely. After a couple of glasses of the wine, Ruby was joining in and smiling, regaling the group with down-home, Southern humor. It also helped that the other three shared two bottles of sake.

Ruby fell asleep on the ride home from the restaurant. Kate shook her gently when she parked and Ruby woke with a start. "We're home. Are you okay?" Ruby looked at Kate with a blank expression like she didn't know where she was. "I'll help you inside." Kate got out of the car and opened the passenger door. She put her arm around Ruby's shoulder and helped her out and then up the front walk to the house. By the time they got to the door, Ruby was able to walk on her own.

"I'm fine now." Ruby wriggled out of Kate's hold on her arm.

Kate wasn't sure what was wrong with Ruby, but she seemed okay now. Crosby greeted them and led the way to Ruby's room. Kate had to admit that she didn't mind having the bed to herself since Ruby had arrived, even if she was jealous that Crosby was choosing Ruby over her as his sleeping partner.

19

RUBY SEEMED TO BE ENERGIZED BY AN EVENING OUT AND SPENT THE NEXT FEW DAYS WORKING WITH KATE IN THE BACK YARD. They planted flowers and shrubs and Kate found that she liked the gardening process as well as the fruits of their labor. She regretted not having done more with the back yard so she could have appreciated it herself instead of just readying it for someone else's enjoyment. As the days went by, she realized that she was going to have to tell Ruby about her plans. Not that she thought Ruby would mind. She seemed to be feeling better or at least she wasn't complaining much. She stopped using the walker or cane, although her pace was very slow. Maybe she was strong enough to go back to Mississippi by now. Kate would make another doctor's appointment for her, and they could discuss it with the doctor.

"I think we need to put in a vegetable garden on that side of the house where the sun is strong." Ruby's comment jolted Kate out of her daydream.

"A vegetable garden?" Kate knew that she wouldn't be staying long enough for that. Flowers and shrubs were for immediate beautification. Planting a vegetable garden was for long-term personal benefit, not to make a house more marketable. "Uh, Ruby? I don't know if we should do that."

"Don't you want to enjoy eating your own vegetables?"

"Well, yeah but . . ."

Ruby looked at her quizzically. "Don't go around your elbow to get to your thumb. Say what you wanna say."

"Let's go inside and talk." Kate put her arm through Ruby's. Ruby shrugged and started to trudge toward the back door. All of a sudden she winced and cried out in pain. "What is it Ruby?"

Ruby shook her head and frowned. "It's getting worse again. The pills aren't working like they used to."

"Oh dear. Well, I wanted to suggest we make another doctor's appointment anyway."

"For what? Doctors are as useless as a screen door on a submarine. They don't do anything but give me medicine and tell me I need that surgery. The medicine doesn't work and I'm not having the surgery."

Kate sighed. "Can you walk, or should I get the wheelchair or the walker?"

"I can walk." Ruby grimaced with each step but she made it to the living room sofa and plopped down. Crosby, of course, immediately jumped on her lap.

Kate sat down next to her. "I think you should see the doctor. I mean, what else can we do?"

"We? This is my pain."

"I just meant — oh never mind."

"I think I'll just lie down. Can you help me into the bedroom?"

"Sure." Kate took Ruby's arm and put her on the bed. "I'll bring you a glass of water and leave it on the nightstand in case you decide to take more pain medication."

"Fine."

Ruby's eyes were closed when Kate returned with the water, and Crosby was curled up next to her, both of them snoring softly. Kate tiptoed out and called Julia to tell her the latest development. "I have to call Charlotte and get the house on the market. I need to tell Ruby what's going on, but now she refuses to see the doctor. She says the pain meds don't work anymore. Sorry to whine like this, Julia, but I'm at my wit's end."

"Your whole life was turned upside down. You have every right to whine!"

"I'm going have to do something pretty quickly. It's going to be time to go to Africa and

127

I really want to get the house sold first. I suppose I could postpone going into the Peace Corps ——"

"Don't even go there, Kate! You've wanted to do this for a long time."

Kate exhaled loudly. "I know."

"Maybe you have to put her in some kind of home."

"You know she'd never do that."

"If she has no choice?"

"She'd just try to leave like she did from the hospital, and then I'd be called back when she falls or passes out or whatever and I'd be right back in the same predicament."

"This is nuts! It's like you're a prisoner."

"Don't remind me."

"There must be something you can do."

"Well, at least I'll call Charlotte. She could come over and see how nice the yard looks and maybe give me a better appraisal. Then I can use that as a way to start the conversation with Ruby. I'll talk to you later. Thanks for lending the ear, Julia." Kate hung up and busied herself in the kitchen. She wanted to use her computer. She should have moved it into her own room, but it gave Ruby something to do too.

After a couple of hours, she went back to Ruby's room and knocked softly. It was getting on to dinnertime and Ruby hadn't even eaten lunch. "Come in." Kate opened the door and saw Ruby sitting at the computer, Crosby asleep on her lap. "Did you want to use the computer?" Ruby asked.

"Uh, if you're finished." Kate smiled. "You're really getting the hang of it, aren't you?"

"I'm learning, but sometimes I have a little trouble reading the screen."

"Here, I can make the font bigger for you." Kate tried to peer at the screen, but Ruby had exited the website before Kate could see what it was. Kate was curious but knew better than to ask. "I'm proud of you."

"Proud of me? Why?"

"Not too many people your age would be willing to learn how to use a computer."

"Well, I'm not like other people."

Kate laughed. "You got that right." Ruby frowned at her. "I'm sorry. I didn't mean to offend you."

"You didn't." Ruby put Crosby gently on the floor and stood. "I think I'll make myself some toast."

"That's all you want for dinner? I can make you something else."

"No. I don't have much of an appetite."

"Is the pain any better?"

Ruby shrugged her shoulders but didn't answer and hobbled out, leaning on her cane.

20

RUBY WAS SITTING AT THE TABLE WHEN KATE ENTERED THE KITCHEN THE NEXT MORNING. There was a pen in her hand and a coffee cup and pad of paper on the table in front of her. "You're up early?" Kate said.

"I made a list. We need to plant some vegetables. It will be faster if you get starters rather than seeds."

"Ruby, I . . . we have to talk."

"Okay. If you don't want vegetables, we can plant some more flowers. But it's time to get them into the ground now."

Kate sighed with relief. She wouldn't have to bring it up first thing this morning. She wanted a couple of cups of coffee to prepare for the uncomfortable discussion they needed to have. "Yeah, more flowers would be nice." Just then the phone rang. Kate answered it. "Hello?" She furrowed her brow. "Uh, yes. She's right here." She looked at Ruby curiously and handed her the phone. "It's for you."

"If it's that doctor I don't want to talk to him."

"It's not."

Ruby took the phone receiver gingerly. "This is Ruby Thomas." A shocked look came over her face. Then in a soft voice she said, "Hello."

Kate poured her coffee and left. She decided to take this opportunity to go on the computer, even though she was dying to know who was on the phone. Ruby had never gotten any phone calls before, but she was also monopolizing the computer lately. Kate needed to do some research into whether or not she could postpone her Peace Corps starting date, just in case.

After about half an hour of web surfing, Kate went back to the kitchen. Ruby was sitting at the table staring out the window. "Are you okay?" She asked.

"What do you mean?"

"You look like you've just seen a ghost." Ruby didn't answer. "You don't have to talk about it if you don't want to."

"I don't."

"Okay. I'm done with the computer if you want to use it."

"What did you want to talk about?" Ruby asked.

"We can talk another time." Kate didn't know what news Ruby had just heard, but she probably wasn't in the mood to hear anymore. "Did you feed Crosby yet?"

"No. I didn't."

Kate poured some dry food into a bowl and put it on the floor. "Here you go, Crosby."

"Thank you," Ruby said softly.

Kate's jaw dropped. "What for?"

"For teaching me how to use the computer."

"Oh. That's okay. I should thank you for making my back yard beautiful. And also for teaching me how to knit."

"You're welcome." Ruby nodded and turned her eyes back toward the window.

Kate took a shower and got dressed. Ruby was still at the kitchen table staring out the window. "Did you write down any specific flowers I should get?"

"Um. No. Just get anything you want."

"Okay. Do you need anything else while I'm out?"

"Are you going to the grocery store?"

"Yes. What do you want?"

"I'll write it down." Ruby squinted and tilted her head as she wrote.

"You really are having trouble seeing. I can buy you a pair of reading glasses at the drug store."

"That would probably be good." Ruby handed Kate the piece of paper.

Kate read it and smiled. "You have a sweet tooth I see. The makings of a chocolate cake?" Ruby nodded and the corners of her mouth rose slightly, but she stayed silent.

When Kate returned a couple of hours later, she found Ruby outside digging while leaning on her walker. It had to be such a struggle to get in and out of the house with that thing, and Kate was always amazed to watch how Ruby did it. But she now knew better than to offer help without being asked. She took the plants outside, and Ruby did seem happy to let Kate take over the digging and planting duties. Ruby's face showed an inkling of pride at how much Kate had learned, even though she would never say so.

That evening they sat side by side on the sofa, watching television, both of them knitting. Crosby lay between them with his head pressing against Ruby's hip and his tail on Kate's lap. They sat in silence for several minutes. Ruby finally spoke. "I'm having a visitor tomorrow."

"A visitor?"

"He'll be here early afternoon."

"He? Is it a suitor?" Kate smiled. Ruby looked at her, bewildered. "Just joking," Kate added quickly. Another few minutes passed in silence. "You don't have to tell me who it is, I guess." Kate put her knitting down and took a sip of tea from her cup on the coffee table.

Ruby started knitting faster and more vigorously. "He's my son."

Kate spat the tea back into the cup, getting some on her shirt. Ruby reached in her pocket, took out a handkerchief and silently handed it to Kate.

Kate dabbed at her shirt. "Your son?"

"I found him on the computer."

"I never knew you had another son!"

"He was Martin's twin."

"What?"

"I said he was Martin's twin."

"Martin never told me."

"He didn't know."

Kate fell back into the sofa. "Jesus!"

Ruby's knitting sped up even more. "Their father was a musician."

"I know. Martin told me that much."

"Their father came to the hospital when Martin and his brother were born. We agreed to split the boys up."

"You what?"

"He took one of the twins, and I took the other."

"My God!"

"I had to."

"I'm not judging you, Ruby. I'm sure you had your reasons."

"We promised we wouldn't have any contact with each other, and I never heard from him."

"In all these years?"

"That's correct."

Kate was silent for a few minutes. Finally she spoke. "So how did your son find you?"

"He didn't. I found him."

"How?"

"On the internet."

"You figured out how to do that on the internet?" Kate shook her head. "You never cease to amaze me, Ruby." They sat in silence, each lost in thought. Neither of them went back to their knitting. Finally Kate spoke. "Where does he live?"

"Los Angeles. He's driving up here tomorrow."

"You must be very excited."

Ruby shrugged. " I don't know."

"Or are you afraid?"

"No."

"Happy?"

"I don't know how I feel. Maybe all of that."

"What does he do? Is he married? Does he have children?"

"I don't know. We just talked briefly." Ruby put her knitting away. "It's getting late. I think I'll go to bed." She stood and reached for her cane, but then decided to leave it and placed it back leaning against the couch. She started walking away slowly, hanging on to the backs of furniture.

"I think you are very brave to do this," Kate said.

"I don't know about that." Ruby left the room.

21

RUBY WAS ALREADY IN THE KITCHEN WHEN KATE ENTERED THE NEXT MORNING. "You're becoming a regular early bird," Kate said as she poured a cup of coffee.

"I didn't sleep too well."

Kate smiled. "I can certainly understand why. This is quite a momentous occasion. By the way, have you tried those magnifying eyeglasses I bought you at the drug store?"

"Yes. They didn't help much. I think there's something else wrong."

"It might be glaucoma. Many people get it as they age."

"Maybe so."

"Mmmmm. I smell chocolate cake."

"Oh dear." Ruby stood and tried to rush over to the oven but had a hard time getting up from the table.

"Let me help you." Kate opened the oven doors and reached for an oven mitt. She took one of the cake layers out of the oven and brought it over to Ruby who touched the top lightly with her finger.

"It's ready."

Kate set it down on the counter and took the other layer out. "What time did he say he'd be here?"

"About one o'clock."

"It's at least six hours from L.A. and that's without traffic."

"He said he'd call if it would be later than that."

"What's his name?"

"Lawrence."

"Did you name him?"

"His father and I named both the boys before they were born."

"Are they identical?"

"I don't know. I never saw him. I didn't want to."

"I can understand that." Kate turned the oven off. "It must have been hard giving him up." Ruby didn't answer. She just turned her head and stared out the window.

Kate left Ruby alone most of the morning. She occasionally asked if there was anything she could do to help, but Ruby was quite adamant that she wanted to make this cake herself. Kate understood and although it was hard to watch Ruby grimace as she worked around the kitchen, she let her.

After Ruby finished icing the cake, she went to her room and closed the door. Kate figured she was taking a nap and tiptoed around. Kate was also nervous about seeing Lawrence. It would be weird if Lawrence looked just like Martin. But she hadn't seen Martin in many years, so she really had no idea what he would have looked like now. She wondered if Lawrence was also gay. That would throw Ruby for a loop.

She also wondered about their father. Martin had never talked about him because he knew nothing about him other than he was a musician. Martin had grown up thinking his father had abandoned him and although he never said so, Kate knew that it must have affected him in some way.

As it got close to one o'clock, Kate wondered if she should knock on Ruby's door. Maybe she was still asleep. But then the door to her room opened, and Ruby came out, dressed in the "good" dress she had worn to the restaurant. Ruby went to the kitchen to finish icing her cake, while Kate went to her room to get dressed. She had a good laugh when she pulled out her "good" jeans to put on. Ruby was sitting on a chair in the living room when Kate emerged. "Shall I put a pot of coffee on?"

"Everything's ready," Ruby replied.

Kate sat down on the sofa. "Do you want your knitting?"

"No."

"Shall I turn on the television?"

"No."

Crosby came in and jumped on Ruby's lap, and Ruby petted him absentmindedly as they sat silently. After a while Kate went into the kitchen and returned. "It's past one-thirty. Do you have a cell phone number for him?"

"No."

"I think I'll go check my email." Just as Kate was leaving the room the phone rang. "Do you want to get it or shall I?"

"You get it."

Kate left and answered the phone in the kitchen. She came back in. "He hit a lot of traffic in San Francisco. He'll be here in about forty-five minutes."

"Okay."

"Are you still going to sit there?"

Ruby stared straight ahead without answering. Kate went back to the computer to check her email.

22

A CAR PULLED UP TO THE FRONT OF KATE'S HOUSE AND A LIGHT-SKINNED BLACK MAN OPENED THE DRIVER'S SIDE DOOR AND GOT OUT. He was attractive and fit, his gray temples the only thing revealing his sixtyish years. A younger black man in his thirties got out of the passenger side and opened the door behind him. He leaned in and took a three-year-old girl out of a car seat, while a black woman in her thirties got out of the back seat on the driver's side. The older man walked up to Kate's front door, while the family of three stayed next to the car. The older man turned around. "Aren't you coming?" The woman picked up the little girl and followed tentatively behind the younger man. The older man rang the bell.

Ruby stood with difficulty and started to walk slowly toward the front door. Kate walked more quickly and got there first, but the look on Ruby's face told her who was going to answer it. Kate shrunk back and stood behind her as Ruby took a deep breath and opened the door.

Ruby and Lawrence stared at each other silently for a couple of seconds, and then Lawrence grinned broadly. "Hello, Mother." Ruby put her hand to her mouth and stifled a sob. Lawrence took her in his arms and hugged her tightly. Kate came forward and gasped when she saw Lawrence. "Do I look that scary?" he said.

"I'm sorry. Not at all, just not what I expected. Come in. Please." Ruby walked back to her chair with her hand still covering her mouth. Lawrence entered and the others followed and sat on the couch. "I'm Kate."

"Yes. I know. You were married to my brother. This is my family: my son, Michael, and his wife, Carla. And this is my granddaughter, Danielle." Michael and Carla smiled while Danielle climbed onto her mother's lap and hid her face in her mother's chest. "Sorry we're late. I thought traffic in Los Angeles was the worst but I think San Francisco may win that prize."

"Yeah, I also think it's worse in San Francisco," Kate replied.

Everyone looked at Ruby who sat motionless. She finally took a deep breath and stood. "Well, this celebration needs a cake. Danielle, would you like to help me bring it in?"

Danielle looked at her mother. "Go ahead, sweetie," Carla said.

Danielle climbed off her mother's lap and walked up to Ruby. She put her hand in Ruby's, and the two walked slowly toward the kitchen. Kate watched Lawrence, Michael, and Carla smile at each other and then joined them. She had a million questions but she should leave those for Ruby to ask. She jumped up to help Ruby with the refreshments, since Ruby was not realistic about what she could and couldn't do. Not only the pain, but also her failing eyesight was starting to get in the way. "Does everyone want coffee?" she asked as Ruby set the cake down on the coffee table.

"Yes," they all answered in unison.

"Do you have any candles?" Carla asked Kate.

"I'm sure I do, but is it someone's birthday?"

"There are a lot of birthdays we've all missed. Why not celebrate them all?"

"That's a great idea." Kate went to the kitchen to retrieve the candles and the coffee.

The animated conversation made the afternoon go by quickly. After eating her cake, Danielle tired of the adult company and played with Crosby on the floor. When she tired of that, or rather when Crosby took refuge on Ruby's lap, Kate set her up at the kitchen table with crayons and paper. She was eager to find out about Lawrence so she hurried back to the living room.

He was a university professor planning to retire soon. He had lived in Los Angeles for thirty years so he was there at the same time Kate lived in Venice. He wanted to write when he retired and Kate spoke of her father, Finn, and how he too had to wait until he retired from teaching before he was able to write his books. Michael and Carla were both teachers so they had a lot in common with Kate and they shared horror stories as well as success stories.

Kate went back to the kitchen to check on Danielle and saw that she was getting sleepy and bored with coloring. "Let's clean up and go back into the living room." Danielle helped Kate put the crayons away before running into the living room to show her parents her masterpiece.

"May I see it too?" Ruby asked. Danielle brought it to Ruby and handed it to her shyly. "This is beautiful. It's Crosby isn't it?" Danielle nodded.

"How did you know it was a picture of Crosby?" Lawrence asked, smiling, as it didn't look much like a cat.

"It looks just like him." Ruby said.

"I'm tired, Mommy." Danielle put her head on Carla's lap.

"I know, honey. Michael, we need to get to the hotel."

"Where are you staying?" Kate asked.

"I don't know. We didn't make any reservations anywhere. Can you recommend a place?" Michael answered.

"Sure. Come with me to the kitchen." Michael followed Kate into the kitchen where they looked up a couple of phone numbers, and Michael made the reservation. Meanwhile Carla brought in the dirty cups and plates. Crosby had settled, as usual, on Ruby's lap and Danielle was petting him vigorously. Lawrence gazed at his mother and granddaughter, smiling with a bit of wistfulness for what could have been.

"Okay. We're all set," Michael said as he returned from the kitchen with Carla and Kate.

Lawrence stood, and Kate saw the look of disappointment on Ruby's face. "Why don't I drive you three to the hotel and Lawrence can stay here with Ruby a little while longer. He can meet you there later."

"Is that okay with you Ruby?" Lawrence asked.

"I'd like that," Ruby smiled.

Michael turned to Ruby. "It was nice to meet you . . . Grandma." He hugged her.

Carla also hugged her and turned to Danielle. "We're leaving now. Say goodbye."

"Bye," Danielle said hanging onto her mother's leg.

"Bye Danielle. Can I have some sugar?" Ruby asked.

Danielle looked up at her mother. "That means she'd like a kiss," Carla said. Danielle ran up to Ruby and gave her a hug and a kiss. Ruby hugged her tightly and tears ran down her cheeks. Kate and Carla also wiped away tears. Kate, Michael, Carla, and Danielle went out the door leaving Ruby and Lawrence standing together, his arm around his mother.

23

RUBY AND LAWRENCE WERE IN THE LIVING ROOM WHEN KATE ENTERED A COUPLE OF HOURS LATER. They were sitting side by side on the couch, but Ruby was asleep with Crosby on her lap. Lawrence put his fingers to his lips and pointed toward the kitchen. Kate nodded and Lawrence stood carefully so as not to wake Ruby, and followed her in.

"You were gone a couple of hours. Is the hotel far?" Lawrence asked.

"I dropped them at the hotel and did a couple of errands. I wanted to give you more time together. I hope that was okay. How long has she been sleeping?"

"Not too long. She told me she had to teach you how to garden." He smiled.

Kate smiled back. "Yes. I guess I had a deprived childhood, growing up in New York City."

"It doesn't sound too deprived. It seems to me your father did a good job raising you alone. Ruby told me some about you."

"She did?"

"Well, I asked."

"I could say the same for you, being raised alone by your father. Professor at UCLA is no small feat."

"Truth be told, I was raised mostly by my grandparents. My father was a musician and he wasn't home much. Besides, he was more interested in women and booze than in taking care of a son. He was too proud to give me back to Ruby, I guess."

"You know, you didn't just have to sit there while she slept. You should have turned on the television or something."

"I didn't mind. I wanted to look at her face. I didn't think I would ever meet her."

"What had your father told you about her?"

"He refused to tell me anything about her. Nor did he tell me I had a twin."

"Well, Ruby never told Martin either, if that's any consolation."

"I'm just glad to meet her now."

"It must have been quite a shock when she got in touch with you."

"Yes it was."

"I think today was pretty overwhelming for her. Did you and Ruby talk about your childhood?"

"Not much. I didn't think she wanted to hear about it."

"You're probably right. Did she tell you about Martin?"

"A little."

"Did she tell you how she treated me when Martin and I were married? And then how she treated Martin after we divorced?" Kate was sorry she had used such a sarcastic tone immediately after she said it.

"She told me the basics. She resented you for being white and Martin for being gay." He put his arm on Kate's shoulder. "But she also said she was sorry and that she had ended up losing both her sons for her stubborn prejudices. And that she appreciated all you've done for her in spite of it."

Kate shook her head. "Nice try. She didn't say that, did she?"

"Okay. Well maybe not. But I think she feels it now. Don't you?"

Kate shrugged and decided to change the subject. "Is Michael's mother around? If you don't mind me asking."

"Dead for many years."

"You never remarried?"

"Nope. You?"

"Nope."

"That's hard to believe. A beautiful woman like you must have had many men chasing after you." Kate looked out the window and didn't answer. "I'm sorry. I didn't mean to pry. It's just that you were still so young with your whole life ahead of you when you and Martin divorced. You never wanted children?"

"It wasn't a conscious decision."

Lawrence realized he was getting into some sensitive territory. "Are you hungry?"

"Famished."

"Let's wake Ruby and see if she wants to get some dinner. My treat." They went back to the living room.

Kate gently tapped Ruby's shoulder. "Ruby?" Ruby's eyes opened and she squinted at Kate and Lawrence for a minute.

"I'd like to take the three of us out to dinner," Lawrence said.

"Oh no. I'm much too tired. I ate too much cake anyway. I'll just go to bed."

Ruby started to push herself up from the couch. Lawrence took her arm to help her up. "This has been a wonderful day."

"I'm glad you brought your family, Lawrence."

"Not just my family; our family." Ruby smiled and Lawrence hugged her tightly. "Will you come down to Los Angeles and visit us?"

"I don't know ——"

"I'll call you this week." Lawrence interrupted before Ruby had a chance to say no.

Ruby nodded. "Goodbye Lawrence." He hugged her tightly and kissed her cheek and she walked slowly down the hall.

Lawrence turned to Kate. "May I take you to dinner?"

"I don't know. I . . . I guess so or I could cook something here."

"I'd like to take you out. You name the place."

"Okay. We can take two cars if you like. Then you can just go to the hotel from there."

"That's not gentlemanly. I'll drive us."

Kate smiled. "Well . . . okay. It's been a while since I've been out with a gentleman."

24

THE RESTAURANT WAS PACKED WHEN KATE AND LAWRENCE ENTERED. "Do you want to try somewhere else?" Kate asked.

"I'm not in a hurry. Are you?"

She smiled. "Not at all. We can wait in the bar." They sat at the bar.

"What would you like to drink?"

"I guess a glass of wine."

"Shall we get a bottle and bring it to the table with us?"

"That sounds good."

"Red or white? Or do you have a specific one that you like when you come here?"

"Whatever you choose is fine with me."

He glanced at the wine list and ordered a bottle of Cabernet. He turned to Kate. "So what was my brother like?"

"It must be incredibly weird to find out now that you had a twin brother."

"Yes, very weird. I just wondered how much alike we are. Or *were*, I guess."

"He was artistic and musical. And kind. Extremely organized. He was politically active when we got together. I don't know about recently. You know why we divorced, right?"

"Because he came out of the closet."

"Correct." Kate took a breath. "I was devastated."

Lawrence put his hand on her arm. "I can imagine." The bartender brought the wine and went through the opening ritual. The hostess came over right then to bring them to their table. After ordering they settled in with their wine and resumed their conversation. "Well, I can attest to being some of those things you mentioned about Martin. But not all."

Kate smiled flirtatiously. "And which things are you not?"

Lawrence smiled back. "I'm politically active, fairly musical, but not that artistic. I'm fairly neat but not that organized and I like to think I'm kind." He looked into her eyes. "I'm definitely not gay."

The flirting continued through dinner and they finished the bottle of wine. The waiter came to clear the plates. "Do you want to see a dessert menu?"

Lawrence looked at Kate who shook her head. "No thanks," Lawrence answered. "We had some good old-fashioned southern chocolate cake earlier today."

"I'll get the check," the waiter answered.

"That was really good cake," Kate said.

"All black women from the south make a mean chocolate cake."

"So your grandmother was also a great baker?"

"Yes. And cook."

"Did your father look like her?"

Lawrence looked at her slyly. "I feel like this is going somewhere in particular."

"I'm looking for the proper way to segue."

"Well, why don't you just come out and say it."

"Okay. Martin had packed a box for me and I got it after he died. In it were some old pictures of the two of us and some letters we had written to each other. But there was other stuff in there too."

"And what was that?"

Kate took a breath. "Did you know that Martin and his father, I mean your father, had corresponded?"

Lawrence was stunned. "No. I didn't."

"When Ruby told me about you and your father, she said that the agreement between them was that there would be no contact."

"That's what she told me when she first emailed me."

"She didn't want you and Martin to know the truth of your circumstances at birth, so your father violated that agreement."

"Apparently he did. But it doesn't really matter at this point."

"Not to you, perhaps."

Lawrence looked at her, perplexed. "I don't understand."

"Your father had sent Martin a picture of himself."

"And?" Lawrence couldn't understand Kate's sudden icy tone.

Just then the waiter arrived with the check. Lawrence took out a credit card and placed it on the bill without looking at it. "Maybe you're right," Kate said. "Maybe it doesn't matter."

"Who would care now? Martin's dead, my father's dead. Ruby and I have met and we are both happy about it."

"I guess it matters to me."

"Tell me. Why would it matter to you?" Lawrence asked, truly confused.

Kate stood. "Maybe you're right. We don't need to go there. Forget it. I need to go to the restroom." Lawrence watched her walk away from the table.

The waiter came back with the credit card slip and Lawrence signed it while Kate was gone. When she returned they went back to the car in silence. Lawrence drove back to Kate's following her directions, but that was the extent of the conversation for several minutes. Finally Lawrence spoke. "I'd like to finish discussing the letters between Martin and my, I mean *our*, father."

"I shouldn't have brought it up."

"It's obviously very important to you. There's more that you're not saying."

Kate turned to him. "Did you ever see a picture of Martin?"

"No."

"You're not identical twins."

"Okay."

"In fact, you don't look alike at all."

"And?" Lawrence asked.

They arrived at Kate's house and she unbuckled her seat belt. "I just thought it was interesting. He's so much darker skinned than you are."

"What are you getting at?"

"I was pretty shocked after seeing the picture of your father."

"Why? Because he was white?"

"Well . . . yeah."

"Why? Because it was the deep South?"

"That too. But more because of the way Ruby treated me when I was married to Martin. She was quite unhappy that he had married a white girl. And yet ——"

Lawrence interrupts. "I'm sure there's a lot about Ruby that you and I don't understand and probably never will."

"You really don't want to know?"

"Not really. It seems like you want to know more than I do." Lawrence replied.

Kate sighed. "I guess that's right. But you have to admit, it doesn't make sense."

Lawrence shrugged. "It doesn't have to for me."

"I wish I could let go of the past that easily."

"It takes some effort."

"Yes, it takes a lot of effort." She exhaled, trying to shake off the old hurts starting to emerge.. "Well, this was quite a day."

"Yes, for everyone."

"I think we'll all need a few days to recuperate and process it all."

Lawrence laughed. "Looks like you've had a bit of therapy."

"Did I really say process? Oh God!" She opened the car door.

Lawrence got out and walked her to the front door. "Maybe you and Ruby could come down to Los Angeles sometime."

"I'm going to South Africa soon."

"South Africa?"

"Yeah. The Peace Corps."

"Wow! When?"

"I haven't told Ruby yet, so please don't say anything. I was waiting for her to be well enough to go home."

"I . . . uh . . ." He shook his head. "I guess I didn't expect this. She's going back to Mississippi then?"

"Did you think she was going to live here with me the rest of her life?"

"I guess I did. I'm sorry. I just wasn't thinking about it at all. You've already done so much for her."

Kate opened the front door and turned back to Lawrence. "Thank you for dinner. Do you remember how to get to the hotel? It's just around the corner from the restaurant."

"You're welcome and yes I remember. I'm really glad I met you, Kate." They gazed at each other for a moment. Then Kate smiled, went inside, and closed the door. Lawrence walked back to his car, got in, and looked back at the house for several minutes before starting the car and driving off.

25

RUBY WAS ALREADY WORKING IN THE BACK YARD WHEN KATE GOT UP THE NEXT MORNING. Kate got her coffee and stood watching through the window as Ruby stopped what she was doing to rub her eyes. She kept blinking and rubbing and finally reached around for her cane. She leaned on it and called out for Kate who rushed out the door. "Kate! Kate! Can you hear me?"

"I'm here, Ruby," Kate said as she approached her. "What's wrong?"

"It's my eyes. I can barely see. It's all cloudy."

"Cloudy? What do you mean?"

"I see flashes and it's like a halo. And a tunnel."

"Do they hurt?"

"Yes."

"They look red. I'll go get your pain pills."

"No. I hate those pills. They make me nauseous and dizzy."

"We'd better go to the doctor."

"Just help me into bed."

"Okay, but then I'm going to call the doctor."

"I'm sick of doctors."

"But you can't see!"

"It will get better."

Kate sighed. "Well, at least take the pain pills."

"I don't want to."

Kate helped Ruby into bed and then went to the kitchen. She looked through some papers piled by the phone and took one out of the pile. She read from it and dialed.

After a couple of hours, Kate tiptoed into Ruby's room. "Are you awake?" she whispered.

"I am now."

"I made an appointment with Dr. Corning for tomorrow morning."

"I said I didn't want to go."

"I know you did, but maybe the problem with your eyes is connected to the heart disease."

"My eyes are better now."

"You need to talk to Dr. Corning."

"I'm not having surgery and that's all he'll say."

"You need to see some doctor, and he's the only one you have here. Let's just see what he has to say." Ruby turned on her side with her back facing Kate. "Call if you need me," Kate said as she left the room.

Ruby stayed in her room most of the day. Kate brought her some lunch and dinner, but she didn't eat much, as usual. Kate wanted desperately to talk about yesterday and how Ruby felt about all that had transpired. She also wanted to talk to her about the future. She realized after talking to Lawrence that her life had been on hold for way too long. She also felt conflicted and confused after meeting him. He had awakened some long dormant feelings: some about her past, but also about her future. And she couldn't deny the attraction for him she felt. He was, after all, the twin of the love of her life.

Ruby probably had some of her own conflicted and confused feelings about meeting Lawrence and his family. One thing at a time, Kate told herself. First find out what's going on with Ruby's eyes and then figure out the next step. Another day wouldn't matter in the grand scheme of things.

26

KATE HELPED RUBY OUT OF THE CAR AND INTO DR. CORNING'S WAITING ROOM. Ruby's pain had kept her up most of the night, but she was adamant about not taking the medicine. She must have felt pretty awful, because Kate found it easy to talk her into going to the nine o'clock appointment. And Dr. Corning must have remembered how stubborn Ruby was, because he came right out to the waiting room himself to bring her into his office. He was probably afraid she would leave if she had to wait.

"She's in a lot of pain and now she's complaining about her eyes," Kate said as they sat down.

"I can speak for myself!" Ruby shot Kate a piercing look.

"So the medication's not working on the pain?" Dr. Corning tried to diffuse things.

Kate looked at Ruby who didn't answer. Kate didn't care at this point and spoke up. "She doesn't want to take it."

"If you're not going to take medicine, Ruby, there's not much I can do for you."

"What about the surgery?" Kate asked.

"No surgery!" Ruby said angrily.

"If it will work, why not?" Kate lashed out.

"The pain is probably more from the broken ribs than the heart problem. Actually, I'm concerned about the surgery now. She's still recuperating from being hit and at her age she's probably not a good candidate."

"So there are no options?"

"The medication would help if she took it. Why won't you?"

"It makes me nauseous and sleepy."

"Are you eating?"

Ruby shrugged so Kate chimed in. "Not much."

"Well, let's concentrate on the eyes now, and I'll do some more research on other medications. I can give you a referral to an ophthalmologist."

"No more doctors!" Ruby exclaimed.

Kate shook her head in disgust. "What do you think is wrong with her eyes?"

"Probably glaucoma."

"Do you think it's connected to the heart disease?" Kate asked.

"It could be connected. There are a few studies indicating that heart disease increases the risk of developing glaucoma. Also African-Americans are significantly more likely to get it."

"Ruby, you need to see an eye doctor."

"I said no more doctors!"

Kate sighed. A couple of minutes went by in silence. Finally Dr. Corning spoke. "They say medical marijuana helps with glaucoma. And it might help with the pain also." He smiled. "But I don't give referrals. You'll have to find a doctor who specializes in that."

Kate smiled back and looked at Ruby out of the corner of her eye, but Ruby showed no emotion. "Well, thanks Dr. Corning. Let's go Ruby." She helped Ruby up and they shuffled out the door.

Ruby went straight to her room when they got home. Kate, meanwhile, went straight to the weekly alternative newspaper to look up ads for medical marijuana clinics or doctors, and for nearby dispensaries. She knew Ruby would probably not do it, but Kate needed to have all the information ready just in case. Ruby might soften if Kate caught her at a moment when the pain was intense, or the eyesight was especially blurred. And maybe she'd at least go to the clinic to see one of the doctors certified to recommend her. Apparently, that's how it worked. Only specific doctors recommended patients for a medical marijuana card. Many doctors didn't want to get involved, because although it was legal under state law in California, it was still illegal under federal law. Kate wrote down the names and phone numbers of a couple of doctors. It sounded simple enough. Now, if she could just convince Ruby. Maybe it wouldn't be that hard. After all, she used to be in the music business. Certainly she must have been around plenty of pot, even if she didn't smoke it.

As she searched for dispensaries, it became clear that there were none in her town. She would have to go into San Francisco. It seemed that only the big cities had dispensaries that you could actually shop at. The smaller towns had delivery services. Getting Ruby to the city would not be an easy task, and Kate wanted to see the selections available. Kate would have to do some more research.

Ruby stayed in her room for most of the day, while Kate decided to go through her closet. She might as well start the process of downsizing. She needed to decide what to take to Africa, what to give away or donate, and what to put in storage. It didn't take nearly as long as she thought it would. She was definitely in the mood to clean out and eliminate.

As she was working, the phone rang. It was Peter. She talked to him for a few minutes and updated him on Ruby's condition as well as the visit from Lawrence. Peter had called to tell her that a friend of Martin's had a guitar that had once belonged to Ruby. Martin had given it to him when he had gotten too sick to play. This friend, Joel, was driving north on his way to Oregon this evening and would like to drop it off for Ruby.

She went to check on Ruby, but she was asleep with Crosby on her stomach. She wanted to kick herself for not moving the computer into her own bedroom. She noticed that it was five o'clock so she went to the kitchen to make dinner.

Ruby ate very little but claimed the pain wasn't that bad. They went to the living room when they finished and sat on the couch to watch television and knit, mostly in silence. Kate had already decided not to bring up the medical marijuana idea tonight. Ruby's pain wasn't excruciating and her eyesight was obviously not that bad or she wouldn't have been able to knit, although she could actually knit without looking. Kate was reminded of that when she glanced over at Ruby and saw that her eyes were closed. Kate, meanwhile, was so unsure of what she was doing that besides looking at her hands intently, she was pressing hard with her fingers on the needles, trying to keep the yarn from unraveling. "My fingers need a break," Kate said as she put her knitting down.

"They'll get used to it," Ruby replied.

"By the way, Peter called today. He wanted to know how you were doing. He also has something of yours."

Ruby opened her eyes and looked at Kate quizzically. "I didn't leave anything at the apartment. What does he have?"

"It wasn't at the apartment. A friend of Martin's had something he thought you should have. He's bringing it here tonight."

"What is it?"

"The guitar you gave Martin many years ago." Ruby stiffened. " Apparently Martin had given it to this guy, Joel, when he had gotten too weak to play it." Ruby put down her knitting needles. "Maybe you can give it to Lawrence if you don't want it," Kate added quickly. Ruby didn't answer; she just stared into space. After a few minutes she picked up her needles and resumed knitting. Kate broke the silence again. "Lawrence and Martin don't look much alike. I guess they're not identical twins."

Ruby stood and put the needles and yarn in her knitting bag. "I'm going to bed. Good night."

"So you don't want to talk about it?" Kate would not let up. She wanted to get her questions answered.

"That's correct. I don't want to talk about it." Ruby started to walk away and just then the doorbell rang.

"Why don't you at least wait to thank Joel for bringing the guitar?" Kate said as she went to the door and opened it.

"Kate?"

"That's me."

"Hi, I'm Joel. Did Peter call you?"

"Yes, this afternoon."

He handed her the guitar case. "Here's the guitar."

"Thank you." She looked at Ruby who said nothing. "Ruby?" Kate felt foolish treating Ruby like a little kid, reminding her that she should thank Joel, but she was angry.

"Thank you," Ruby mumbled as she hobbled down the hall to her bedroom.

"I've got to run. I'm trying to at least get to Redding tonight before stopping at a motel. It's nice to meet you. Martin spoke a lot about you."

"He did? After all these years?" Kate asked.

"You were a very important person in his life." Joel smiled. "One time, after a few drinks, he said to me, 'Kate and I would have had beautiful children.' That always stuck with me. Now that I've met you, I couldn't agree more."

Kate smiled. "Safe travels." She closed the door and picked up the guitar case. She walked down the hall and knocked on Ruby's door.

"Yes?" Ruby said.

Kate opened the door and walked in. "I'll just leave this here." She leaned the guitar against the wall and waited for a minute to see if Ruby would say anything. She didn't so Kate left, closing the door behind her with just a little bit more force than was necessary.

27

KATE WAS ON HER SECOND CUP OF
COFFEE BY THE TIME RUBY ENTERED
THE KITCHEN. "Good morning, Ruby. Shall
I pour you some coffee?"

"Okay."

"How about breakfast? You slept a long
time yesterday and didn't eat much."

"I'm not sleeping all that time. It's just
more comfortable lying down."

"Is the pain worse?"

"About the same."

"What about your eyes?"

"Not good."

"Is it tunnel vision?"

"Something like that."

Kate took a deep breath; she was always
wary when bringing things up to Ruby. "Maybe
it's time to try the marijuana."

"I'm not going to break the law."

"It's legal in California for medicinal
purposes. You just have to get a certain doctor
to recommend it and then you get a card of
some sort."

"I've never smoked a day in my life and I'm not going to start now!"

"You don't have to smoke it. You can eat it in brownies or cookies or other stuff. Maybe there are even pills you can take. Let's just find out about it before you say no."

"I don't like the pain pills so I probably won't like that either."

Kate let out an exasperated sigh. "All right, Ruby. I can't make you."

"That's right. You can't."

"So what do you want for breakfast?"

"Just toast."

Kate busied herself making the toast and pouring coffee. The phone rang just as she set the plate down in front of Ruby. "Hello?" She grinned. "Hi Lawrence. Ruby's right here. Hold on a min— Oh, okay." Kate glanced at Ruby. "Well she's eating her breakfast now anyway so we can chat until she's done."

Ruby watched Kate as she talked, and noticed that the smile never left her face. When Kate noticed that Ruby was staring at her, she took the phone into the living room. Ruby had just finished her toast when Kate came back in and handed her the phone. "Hello Lawrence," Ruby said and she couldn't help but beam either.

Kate went back to the living room to give Ruby privacy and returned when she didn't hear her talking anymore. She sat down across from Ruby. "He wants you to visit him in Los Angeles."

"I know."

"I'll bring you down there."

"Maybe."

"Ruby, we need to talk."

"I said I would think about getting the marijuana!" Ruby exclaimed irritably.

"Not that. Something else."

"What?" Ruby squirmed and rubbed her eyes.

"Would you be more comfortable on the sofa?"

"Yes."

Kate helped her to the living room. It was probably better to have this conversation in there, anyway. Ruby could knit while they talked and maybe she'd be more relaxed. Kate brought her the knitting bag and Crosby started playing with the ball of yarn so it took awhile to get her settled and to divert Crosby's attention. Finally Kate tried again. "Before Martin died I had applied to the Peace Corps. I was accepted to go to South Africa." She cleared her throat. "I need to sell the house before I go."

"So?"

"So . . . what will you do?"

"It's time for me to go home anyway."

"Oh Ruby. You can't live by yourself."

"Sure I can."

"You need to be realistic. Your eyesight is getting worse by the minute. You could have another heart attack at any time. You can't do it."

"Then I'll get that marijuana."

"First of all, it's not legal in Mississippi; it's legal in just a few states. And the marijuana might lessen the pain and help with some of the symptoms of the glaucoma, but it's only going to make you a bit more comfortable, not cure you."

"I've lived alone all this time. I'll be fine."

"Ruby, please. You won't be fine. I'm sorry to be so blunt, but it's true." Ruby sighed and looked away. "I thought maybe we could ask Lawrence if you could live with him," Kate said in a soft voice.

Ruby kept knitting without saying a word. Kate sat quietly and petted Crosby to keep him from disturbing the ball of yarn. Finally Ruby answered. "I'll think about it."

Kate got up. "Okay." She left Ruby to her thoughts and went to take advantage of Ruby's absence from her room to use the computer. She got all the information she could find about the local clinics and dispensaries. She checked prices for airline tickets to Los Angeles. She went to Zillow to see what her house might be worth now and then emailed Charlotte. It felt good to be back on her own path.

Two hours had elapsed by the time she got up to check on Ruby. Crosby had unraveled most of the work Ruby had done during those two hours, but Ruby's eyes were closed and she hadn't noticed. Kate started to walk into the kitchen when she heard her name called. "Kate, could you come here a minute."

"Sure." Kate sat down.

"I do want to try the pot."

"I think it's a good decision. I'll call for an appointment with a doctor for the referral."

Kate called one of the clinics she had written down and was able to get Ruby in for an appointment the following morning. She took Ruby out to the backyard to do some sprucing up. Ruby shouted orders at Kate who did the work, but that was fine. Ruby couldn't see well enough unless she was right next to a plant and standing directly over it. Kate had to walk her from plant to plant, and the whole excursion ended up taking the entire afternoon. They both took a nap before dinner.

After dinner Kate called Charlotte to set up a meeting for the following afternoon. Then she joined Ruby in front of the television for another knitting lesson, although most of her time was spent keeping Crosby away from the yarn skeins. Ruby's mood seemed uplifted. Kate wasn't sure why. Was it the prospect of the marijuana working? Or the phone conversation with Lawrence? But Kate took advantage of her raised spirits and openness by asking a few questions. Her interest in Lawrence piqued her fascination with Ruby's background.

"Have you picked up the guitar yet?"

"You mean the one that Martin's friend left?"

"Yes. What other one would I mean?"

"Don't have to be snippy."

"Sorry."

"No. It's been a long time since I've played."

"Were you good?"

"Good enough."

"Martin had told me that you taught him to play, but I assumed you just knew the basics and that he had taught himself the rest."

"He did teach himself a lot when he was a child."

"I wonder if Lawrence plays too. He said he was somewhat musical, but he didn't specify what instrument he played or if he just meant he liked music."

"I don't remember him saying that."

"It was when we were at dinner, after you had gone to sleep."

"Oh." Ruby continued to knit quietly. After a few minutes she asked, "What else did he tell you about himself?"

Kate smiled. She was surprised that Ruby would actually ask questions. "He said he wasn't artistic . . . just musical. Um . . . that he was politically active . . . oh and that he was kind, but we already knew that from meeting him. He had all that in common with Martin." Kate glanced at Ruby from the corner of her eye. "But he did add that he was not gay. I guess we already knew that, too."

Ruby put her knitting down and picked up Crosby to put on her lap. "Did he say anything about his father?" She petted Crosby more intensely.

"He said he wasn't around much, always on the road with his band. Lawrence was raised moistly by his grandparents."

"That was probably best. They seemed like good people."

"You met them?"

"Once. At the hospital."

Kate debated about telling Ruby what she had found out about Martin corresponding with his father. Not now. Ruby had been more agreeable and forthcoming than she had ever been. Kate didn't want to spoil that. She decided to change the subject. "The real estate lady is coming tomorrow afternoon, after we get back from the clinic."

"What for?"

"To reassess the value of the house since we landscaped the back yard." She turned to Ruby and put her hand on her arm. "Thank you for that."

Ruby nodded and took up her knitting again, and Kate picked hers up as well. The only sound was the click of the knitting needles and Crosby's purring.

28

THE RECEPTION AREA IN THE CLINIC WAS SMALL, LOW-LIT AND ZENLIKE WITH FERNS AND SOFT INDIAN SITAR MUSIC PLAYING. A wind chime hung by the front door announcing the arrival of Ruby and Kate. A woman in a long, flowing dress entered from a back room. She bowed her head and put her hands together. "Namaste. May I help you?"

Ruby looked bewildered. Even Kate had to admit that this was not your usual medical office, but for Ruby this was not even on her radar.

"This is Ruby Thomas," Kate answered.

"Yes. We were expecting you. Come with me, Ruby." The woman smiled at Kate. "You can wait here."

"She may need help walking. She's in pain and —"

"I can walk," Ruby interrupted.

Kate put her hands up in surrender. "Okay." She sat down and opened a *High Times* magazine, pretending to read it. Ruby followed the woman, walking slowly, leaning on her cane. Kate wondered if this doctor had a regular practice as well. It certainly didn't seem like your typical doctor's office. The waiting room was not full. The odor of Naugahyde and rubbing alcohol was not pervasive. It was certainly not a bad place to bide one's time. She leaned back, closed her eyes and let her mind wander while she listened to the music and smelled the lavender incense.

Ruby was back in the waiting room in a matter of minutes. "That was quick," Kate said, sitting up quickly. "I guess the doctor just took your word for it. You don't look like a major stoner!" Kate laughed at her own joke, but neither Ruby nor the receptionist joined in.

"Ruby needs to bring in proof of California residency and a note from her doctor describing her diagnosis."

"She doesn't have a driver's license."

"Maybe she has a bank statement or a utility bill? Something mailed to her address with her name on it. And she will also need a picture ID."

Kate hadn't thought about all that. Now what? She supposed she could open a bank account for her and take her to the DMV for a California State Identification Card. This was getting out of hand. And Kate wasn't even sure

Ruby would follow through. "Uh, okay. How long will it take after that to get the referral?"

"We could give it to her the same day."

"And then would we be able to call the delivery service that day?"

"I'm sorry but I can't give you any information about that."

"What do you mean?"

"You can look online or in ads in the newspaper."

"Why can't you give me information about where to buy it?"

"Regulations."

"Really? That seems ridiculous."

"I'm sorry. It's not our choice."

"But it's legal."

"Yes. In the state but not with the federal government."

Kate and Ruby walked out and got into the car. "What are we going to do?" Ruby asked.

"I'm not sure. We'll have to figure it out."

"And isn't it a prescription? What's this referral thing? And why can't we buy it there? What did she mean?"

"I read that online. The doctor just recommends that you use it for a condition. They can't actually prescribe it because of federal regulations. I hope there's no waiting period or something. I guess I'll have to find a delivery service myself, since there are no dispensaries here."

"You mean you don't just go to a drug store?"

"No. The big cities have dispensaries where you can go to buy it, but here it's just a delivery service."

"But I don't know what I want."

"I'm guessing that the delivery service brings a bunch of stuff to you and explains how much to take. There are lots of choices, Ruby. Don't worry. We'll figure it all out."

They drove the rest of the way home in silence. Kate sensed that Ruby was nervous and maybe a little scared. She had experienced an awful lot of unfamiliarity and stress. Her heart condition, broken ribs, and fast developing blindness was bad enough, not to mention the grief over losing a son, and the anxiety of meeting the one you gave up sixty years ago.

Ruby went straight to her bed to take a nap, which meant Kate had to wait to go on the computer and search for information on the DMV website and a delivery service. She called Julia and as Kate expected, Julia had some information on the delivery service. She seemed to know something about everything. "I've heard that the delivery service is simple to use.

They're available immediately and they are very knowledgeable. It's not cheap, though."

"I've already accepted that fact. I just hope it works. Once she's feeling a little better, I can make my plans."

"You mean send her home?"

"She can't live alone. I'm hoping that she can move in with Lawrence."

"Have you asked him yet?"

"I've brought it up to Ruby. I think she should be the one to ask. But she didn't really respond. I haven't broached the subject with Lawrence yet."

"Don't you think that would be what you'd do first?"

"I think I already know that he would do it. He's a kind-hearted man who just met his mother for the first time. Why wouldn't he?"

"Do I detect some interest other than platonic?"

"Oh Julia, for heaven's sake! I'm about to go in the Peace Corps for two years, and who knows what I'll do after that. It's hardly the time for me to kindle a romance."

"You didn't answer my question."

Kate didn't want to answer Julia's question. If she did, she would have to admit the truth to herself. She had always been better at avoiding introspection than at facing it. "Just leave it alone, Julia."

"You just answered it. Ha!"

"Thanks for the information on the delivery service. I'll talk to you later." Kate hung up and found that she was not going to be successful at putting Lawrence out of her mind.

Kate did some cursory cleaning up. Charlotte would be there in less than an hour. She wanted to wake Ruby now to give her enough time to make herself presentable. Kate had a feeling that Ruby would want to wear her "good" dress for the occasion. Kate actually looked forward to showing Charlotte how much the backyard had changed. She was beginning to understand how gardening was therapeutic for people. One felt a tremendous sense of accomplishment and pride in watching the transformation. Ruby did, in fact, want to wear her Sunday best for Charlotte's visit. But before she got dressed, she made Kate take her outside for one last look around.

Charlotte's visit was very short. She admired the backyard and upped the asking price thirty thousand. After all the papers were signed, Charlotte asked, "Are you ready to list it?"

Kate looked at Ruby but got a blank face in response. She was on her own to answer. "I guess. But nobody will just show up without calling first. Right?"

"Absolutely. In fact, you can require twenty-four hour notice if you want."

"No. That's okay. I just want to know when they're coming."

"First I will bring the local realtors in on our weekly MLS tour. Will tomorrow morning be okay for that?"

Again Kate looked at Ruby who showed no emotion so she answered, "Sure."

"Ten?"

"Sure."

Charlotte left, and Kate went to the computer to look up California Identification Card information and marijuana delivery services. She knew she would have to lend Ruby the money to open a bank account. And then they would have to wait until they sent her an ATM card or something, so she would have her address on the envelope.

Ruby went to the living room to watch television and scold Crosby for continually unraveling her ball of yarn. Kate joined her after dinner, and the evening was another quiet knitting circle, both women lost in thought.

29

BREATHLESS, AFTER A PARTICULARLY VIGOROUS EARLY MORNING JOG, KATE ENTERED THE KITCHEN AND POURED HERSELF A CUP OF COFFEE. She looked up to find Ruby standing in the doorway. Kate wanted to give Ruby the spiel on getting the identification card and the bank account and how to go about getting marijuana legally from the delivery service, but she was hesitant. She had already phoned Dr. Corning who was happy to give her some paperwork on the diagnosis. It was enough of an ordeal that Kate wondered why she didn't just find a dealer. She could certainly ask several of her friends and acquaintances. After all, she lived a hop, skip, and a jump from the Emerald Triangle: the region in northern California that is the largest cannabis-growing area in the world. But she also knew that Ruby would never do it except the legal way. "Can I make you some eggs for breakfast?" Kate asked.

"Just coffee."

"I know you're not hungry, but you eat so little." Ruby just glared at her and Kate got the message. "How are you feeling?"

"The same."

"How about the eyesight?"

"The same. Maybe worse. It's kind of hard to tell unless I'm trying to read or focus on something."

"Well, I did check out delivery services. They'll come here and explain it to you before you buy anything."

"Explain what?"

"The various ways to take it."

"I'll just get cookies or something like that."

"Okay, but they still need to explain how much to take."

"You don't just eat a cookie?"

"You have to see how it affects you. You start with a small amount and see how it's working. It also takes longer to work, I think, when you eat it."

"Longer than what?"

"Smoking."

"Well, I'm not smoking it."

"I know. I just thought you might want to hear all the alternatives."

"Can't you just go out and get me some cookies?"

"I think you have to designate me as a caregiver." Kate wondered if that might not be easier, but then realized that Ruby couldn't designate her until she, herself, got the referral. Maybe Kate should just make up an illness and do the whole thing herself. But then, what would happen when Kate left? "I won't always be here, Ruby."

Ruby nodded. "Yes. I know you want to leave."

Kate wanted to crawl into a hole. That woman had such a way of making her feel like shit. "These were my plans for years. I retired just for that purpose."

"You don't have to defend them. I just said that I know that's what you want."

"Then have you thought anymore about asking Lawrence if you can live with him?"

"I've thought about it."

"And?"

"And what? I've thought about it."

Kate sighed. God! This woman was so exasperating! "Shall I ask him if you don't want to ask him yourself?"

Ruby shrugged. "Up to you."

Kate realized that Ruby was afraid to ask and she didn't mind at all having an excuse to call Lawrence. "Okay. But you know, there's no rush. It's not like the house will sell tomorrow and my start date for the Peace

Corps isn't for a month or two." Ruby just nodded and Kate left it there. She would wait to call Lawrence until after the realtors left in the morning and while Ruby was taking a nap.

It didn't take the realtors very long to size up the house. They were quite impressed with the backyard, and Kate could see the pride in Ruby's face when they oohed and aahed. As expected, Ruby took a nap after they left. Kate settled into the living room sofa with the phone and a cup of tea to make the call to Lawrence.

They talked for more than an hour. Lawrence seemed genuinely interested in everything Kate brought up and was open to any and all questions she had for him. He was also happy to bring Ruby into his home, although he said he would talk to Michael and Carla about having Ruby live with them. They had a house with a lovely yard, while Lawrence lived in a condo. And Kate and Lawrence agreed that it would be nice for both Ruby and Danielle to be with each other full time.

They talked about Kate's father, Finn, and his books. Lawrence had heard of them but hadn't read them. He said he would order them as soon as they got off the phone. Kate explained why she chose to teach at a girls' school in Africa for her two year Peace Corps stint. Lawrence spoke of his own long, academic career as a professor. He answered a few preliminary questions about his first wife, but Kate found that she really didn't want to hear that much about her.

Kate was eager for Ruby to wake up. She wanted to share her conversation with Lawrence and the news that he would be glad to have her move down to southern California, and that he would talk to Michael about Ruby moving in there. She also wanted to see if Ruby was ready to start the process of getting the referral. Kate was beginning to see a light at the end of this long, frustrating tunnel.

Ruby woke up and had a cup of soup. Kate couldn't understand how someone could exist on the tiny amount of food Ruby ate. She assumed that people's metabolism changed when they got older, but her father was about the same age as Ruby and he had a healthy appetite for both food and whiskey. Ruby had lost interest in the medical marijuana when Kate described the ordeal it would take to get it. Her interest was renewed, however, when she tried to knit in front of the television that afternoon and found that she couldn't see well enough to do either. Her pain had also gotten worse.

30

THE PHONE RANG OFF THE HOOK THE NEXT MORNING WITH REALTORS EAGER FOR APPOINTMENTS TO SHOW THE HOUSE. This was not what Kate had expected. She thought her house was small, having only two bedrooms, and overpriced. She hadn't realized that the areas north of San Francisco were valued just as outlandishly as the city itself. It would be a busy day today with the parade of visitors, and she wondered how Ruby would do with all this excitement, not being able to get her nap in.

Kate called a few marijuana collectives and found one of them willing to deliver as soon as they received a copy of the referral from the doctor and a form of identification. After a few more phone calls and an extensive Google search, Kate became discouraged again. It would take at least thirty days for the paperwork to be done, so that Kate could then be listed as a caregiver and use her Medical Marijuana Identification Card. This was getting far too complicated and time-intensive for what

Kate thought (or at least hoped) would be a quick fix. And then it would be just a short time until Ruby would be moving to Los Angeles, and she'd have to go through finding a place down there and possibly designating Lawrence, Michael, or Carla as a caregiver.

Ruby entered the kitchen just as Kate had finished dialing Lawrence's number. She hung up quickly. She wasn't ready to share all this with Ruby after having worked so hard to convince her to try the marijuana. She decided to call Julia and Lucy instead and see if they could meet for coffee. Even if they didn't have any answers, they could at least be sounding boards for Kate.

"Coffee?" Kate asked Ruby as she sat down.

"Okay."

"There will be a few people looking at the house today," Kate said as she poured the coffee.

"I'll stay out of their way."

"Don't worry about that. You just go about doing whatever you want to do. It just may be hard for you to get a nap in."

"I'll manage."

Kate went to her bedroom to call Julia and Lucy and they agreed to meet in half an hour. Kate postponed her shower until after she got back. The first appointment was at noon, so there would be time when she got home from the cafe. She got dressed and went back to the kitchen. "I'm meeting Julia and Lucy. I'll be back in an hour. No one is coming until noon to look at the house."

"Okay."

Kate left Ruby staring out the window, wincing with pain. Kate wondered if Ruby could even see the fruits of her labor in the backyard anymore, unless she was standing right on top of them.

Julia and Lucy were already seated at the cafe when Kate arrived. She got a cappuccino and sat down. "So what's the emergency?" Julia asked.

Kate brought them up to date, and they sat silently listening. Julia was biting at the bit to interrupt, but she could tell that Kate really wanted to vent and unload. This was not just about the trials and tribulations of getting medical marijuana in the state of California. It was about all that Kate had been enduring since that fateful phone call from Peter many weeks ago.

After more than twenty minutes of ranting, Kate slumped back in her chair and sighed. And that's when Julia took the cue and jumped in. "Why don't you do what everybody else I know does and just buy some pot. I can hook you up with some people who grow it and sell it."

"Ruby would never acquiesce to that. It took me forever to convince her that it was in fact legal here."

"Most of my friends get the doctor's referral so that if they ever get stopped by the police, they won't get arrested. But they don't buy it at dispensaries because it's too expensive. Anyway, Ruby is just going to be doing it at your house. She's not going to be driving around with it in her purse."

"I know but she would never agree. Anyway, she doesn't want to smoke it. She wants to eat it like in a cookie or something."

"There are lots of other alternatives to smoking. What about a vaporizer? Or you can just buy it and make your own cookies or brownies."

"How do you know so much?" Lucy asked.

Julia smiled. "Been doing it for years."

"How come we never knew that about you?" Kate asked.

"It just never came up."

"Do you do it for a particular reason or just to get high?"

"Depression, anxiety, insomnia. I use a vaporizer. I do Sativa in the morning and Indica at night."

"You do realize that we don't know what you're talking about," Lucy said.

"You two used to smoke pot in college didn't you?" They both nodded. "Well it's gotten a lot more sophisticated and potent since those days when getting high meant being hungry, giggling a lot, and falling asleep. If you're interested, Kate, I can go over some of the various kinds and how they differ from each other. Then you can decide what you want to do, and I'll even get it for you so you won't have to meet any of these big bad criminals."

Kate and Lucy both laughed. "Okay," Kate answered. "But I have to get home and get my house ready for what I hope will be an onslaught of prospective home buyers who are coming this afternoon."

"How about dinner tonight at my house?" Lucy asked.

"Sure."

"Maybe you should bring Ruby, so she can hear about the different kinds."

"I told you, Julia, she'd never agree to getting it illegally."

"She should know about the different kinds. Then you could just pretend that you're getting it for her legally."

"But I already told her about the delivery service and — "

"Really Kate!" Julia said impatiently. "You can think of something."

Kate smiled. "You're right. I can. What time, Lucy?"

"Six."

31

THERE WERE THREE BACK-TO-BACK APPOINTMENTS TO SHOW THE HOUSE AND SEVERAL PEOPLE STAYED FOR A LONG TIME. Ruby stayed in her room and Kate worked in the garage, organizing and throwing more things away. It was quite energizing and cleansing, although she did have some melancholy moments. After the last group left the house, Kate realized that she hadn't told Ruby about their dinner plans. Maybe that was subconscious. Kate was a bit ambivalent about the lying and sneaking, but the alternative was worse. She knocked on Ruby's door. "I'm sorry. I forgot to tell you. We are both invited to Lucy's for dinner."

"When?"

"Tonight. Actually we have to leave in fifteen minutes." Ruby was silent. "Is that okay?"

Ruby finally answered after about thirty seconds. "Yes."

Kate was surprised, but actually thankful that Ruby agreed. Somehow it felt like Julia was taking some of the burden of Ruby off Kate's shoulders. Lawrence did too in welcoming Ruby to live with him. Maybe things were finally falling into place and Kate could go forward with her plans, as long as she kept suppressing her growing fondness for Lawrence.

Lucy had cooked a southern-influenced meal for Ruby, but with a California twist: fried chicken and greens but cooked in locally grown olive oil instead of bacon fat, cornbread but served with a homemade plum jam, and peach cobbler for dessert. They had California wine, but a Riesling to accommodate Ruby's sweeter taste. And Julia waited until Ruby had finished her first glass of wine and was well into her second before beginning her marijuana lesson.

"Kate told us that you are interested in trying medical marijuana, Ruby. I've been using it for years for depression and insomnia. And for pain."

Kate glanced furtively at Ruby to see her reaction. She didn't change her facial expression, nor did her body stiffen. Kate breathed a sigh of relief, although she wondered if maybe Ruby hadn't heard her. Kate pretended to be surprised. "I didn't realize that. Maybe you can help us sort out the different ways to take it and the various types. It's very confusing."

"Sure." Julia played along.

"Smoking is the fastest way for it to work, and it's also easier to adjust the dose."

"I don't smoke and don't want to start now," Ruby stated adamantly.

"I don't like to smoke it either. I use a vaporizer. It takes out all the harmful toxins."

"Is that like an asthma inhaler?" Lucy asked.

"Kind of," Julia answered, "but it's not quite that simple. You still have to heat it, just not as much as you would if you smoked it."

"That sounds like too much trouble," Ruby interjected.

"Okay. Well, then you can drink it like tea, but you have to steep it a long time. I've never done it, but I've heard that you would add butter to it to enhance it."

"Butter?"

"Apparently, the tea isn't very potent unless you add the butter."

"That doesn't seem too easy either," Kate added. " I would think eating it in cookies or something like that would be best for Ruby."

"That may be true but there are two things you have to know. One is that it takes longer to work than smoking or vaporizing."

"Like how long?"

"An hour or two."

Kate looked at Ruby. "You'd just have to be patient waiting for it to work."

"Most people aren't patient, so they end up taking more and then they take too much."

Kate's first reaction was a little pissed at Julia for bringing up any problems with it at all. She was so sure Ruby would look for ways to get out of taking it and then wouldn't feel well enough to make the move to Lawrence's. But Ruby didn't reject it at all. In fact she asked several questions, much to Kate's surprise.

"So how do you know how much to eat? And how does it make you feel? Am I going to be high?"

"I need to explain how the two kinds are different. One is called Cannabis Indica and the other is called Cannabis Sativa. The ingredients in both of them are THC and CBD. It's the amount of each in the two strains that makes them different in what they're used for and how they make you feel. THC is what makes you high. CBD treats certain ailments but doesn't make you high."

"So I would want CBD."

"Well, it's not that simple. You have to figure out which one works best for your particular problem. And there's a hybrid that is a cross between the two. That's why the hybrids are good. The combination, hopefully, will take care of what you need without making you too stoned."

"So which one is in Indica and which is in Sativa?" Kate asked.

"It's not that one is all THC and one is all CBD. They are different plants."

"Huh?" Ruby and Kate both asked.

"I'm sorry if I made it sound like it was one or the other. Both plants have both THC and CBD of varying degrees."

"So then what's the point of having a hybrid?" Kate asked.

Julia took a sip of wine and put up her finger as if to say, "Wait a minute." She needed to figure out how to explain marijuana to people who hadn't been smoking pot for the last forty years. Kate and Ruby sat quietly, while Lucy went into the kitchen and started doing the dishes. "Hey Lucy!" Julia yelled toward the kitchen. "Where can I find some paper to write on?" Lucy entered with a yellow legal pad and handed it to Julia. "Thanks."

"Why can't I just ask that doctor and ask what to do?"

Kate looked at Julia. She couldn't let Ruby know their plan to just get it on the black market. "They won't tell you anything helpful," Julia answered quickly. "But listen, Ruby. I do know all about it. Do you want me to just tell you what to take, and then Kate can get it for you?"

"I thought she had to —"

"Maybe that would be the best way! " Kate interrupted.

Ruby was silent. Kate knew exactly what was going on in Ruby's mind. Here she goes again: Kate trying to take over. Kate waited to see if Ruby would say anything. Finally she did. "Okay. Go on. Explain."

Julia shook her head and drew a picture on the pad of paper. "This is an Indica plant." She drew a short bush. "It has more CDC and less THC so you don't get energized. Instead you get sleepy and relaxed. I use it at night for insomnia." She drew a tall, thin plant with narrow leaves. "This is a Sativa plant. It's more THC and less CDC so it's a stimulant, good for depression. I take it in the morning."

"You use both?" Kate asked, this time truly surprised.

"Not every day. Well, most days."

"So basically, for as long as I've known you, you've always been stoned?"

Julia looked at Kate sharply. "Are you being judgmental?"

"No. I just didn't know that about you." Then Kate realized what she was saying in front of Ruby. Damn. Too much wine and loose lips. She was doing exactly what she didn't want Julia to do, turn Ruby off to the idea. She quickly offered up a counter. "That just goes to show that using it medicinally doesn't make you stoned or high, necessarily," she said looking at Ruby.

"Just tell me what I should get." Ruby was now exasperated with both of them.

"Yes. Which one is best for pain and glaucoma?" Kate asked.

"I did my homework. I talked to some people and did some research. I think the best one for Ruby would be Maui Waui."

Ruby burst out laughing. Kate soon joined in. Julia smiled. She expected that response. Kate finally asked, "So is it Indica or Sativa? Is Ruby going to run around like the Duracell bunny or go to sleep?"

"I don't think either. I think she'll like it. It's a strain of Sativa."

"That's the one that has more THC?"

"Just forget all that stuff. Try it. If you don't like it, there are others to try."

"What do you say Ruby?"

"Can I buy a cookie made from it?"

Kate looked at Julia. "You know, Ruby, I just happen to have some. I baked cookies for you to taste. You would just start with a quarter of a cookie. See how you feel after an hour and a half. Then just take a little more if it hasn't helped." Julia looked at Kate now. "But be careful not to eat a lot more if you don't feel anything."

"We get it, Julia." Kate exclaimed. She spoke before Ruby could change her mind.

Julia took out a small Ziploc bag with two cookies inside. "Eat it tomorrow morning. I don't want it to keep you up all night."

Ruby hesitated for a moment and then took the bag. "Thanks."

Kate expected Ruby to question the legality of it, or whether there would be any repercussions for the fact that this wasn't bought at a dispensary or through the delivery service. But Ruby seemed quite content to trust Julia's baking abilities and marijuana knowledge. Ruby quickly stuck the bag in her purse. Kate breathed easily and poured more wine into both Julia's and Ruby's glasses. "You joining us Lucy?" she called out to the kitchen.

"Here I am." Lucy sat down and Kate poured some into Lucy's glass as well. Kate left her own empty. After all, she designated herself the driver and told Julia as much. Julia didn't protest, and the night that Kate worried would be a complete disaster became an evening of laughter and merriment.

32

KATE WAS UNABLE TO SLEEP THAT NIGHT. Her mind was racing. Her plans were finally coming to fruition. She would sell the house, do her two-year Peace Corps stint, and be free to take whatever next step presented itself on life's journey. And Ruby would be taken care of. She had to admit that she had actually started to grow fond of her, even if she still had trouble reconciling Ruby's treatment of her and Martin. But Ruby had produced two incredible men. How bad could she be? So why did insomnia visit her when things were finally going her way? She felt like a huge burden had been lifted; her stress level had become much more manageable. But there was a lot to organize and life changes, even when chosen and welcome, were still challenging. And she had to stop trying to fool herself; she had also grown rather fond of Lawrence. That was unexpected and threw a wrench in her plans. It made leaving even more problematic.

Kate gave up trying to fall asleep and finally got out of bed at five. She debated about making coffee, since that would cement the fact that she was up for the day. She decided that she could always take a nap later if she needed to, so what the hell. She made the coffee, read the paper, wandered around the house, but realized that there wasn't much she could do at that hour because she didn't want to wake Ruby.

At six she decided to call her father in New York. He was probably up at nine and he needed to be updated. She hadn't talked to him in a couple of weeks, and the last time they had, things were very unsettled and unresolved. She liked to be able to give him some good news for a change. He would enjoy hearing that she had met a man she actually cared about. And he would get a kick out of hearing about Ruby's latest foray into the world of medicinal marijuana. After all, Finn was no stranger to the bottle and other forms of self-medication. And he had known Ruby as the God-fearing, southern Baptist who couldn't handle a white daughter-in-law. He would be amused.

She and her father talked for almost an hour. He was a healthy, spry man in his eighties — a far cry from Ruby. He and Kate had a complicated relationship, and it had fluctuated through the years between living together and not speaking for months at a time. But it had mellowed the last fifteen years into a relaxed, communicative rapport that didn't rely on the quantity of time they spent together. There was no guilt on either side when weeks or even months passed without a phone call and years without a visit. It had taken many years and soul-searching to reach this point.

After she hung up with her father, she made some oatmeal and was just finishing breakfast when Ruby walked into the kitchen. "Would you like some oatmeal? I made plenty."

"Just coffee."

"Do you want to try the cookie with your coffee? A quarter of a cookie shouldn't be difficult to get down, even if you don't have an appetite."

"I guess I'll try it."

Kate took the cookie out of the Ziploc bag and broke off a piece. "It looks good. Chocolate chip I guess." She handed it to Ruby.

Ruby took the cookie and smelled it. She wrinkled her nose. "It smells bad."

"Well, it might not be the best chocolate chip cookie you ever ate, but I assume it isn't too terrible." Ruby took a miniscule bite. "You have to eat more than that." Ruby put the whole piece in her mouth and chewed it. "So?"

Ruby gave a small shrug and swallowed. "I've eaten worse."

Kate sighed with relief. "Okay. Now we just wait and see how you feel in an hour. Are you in much pain this morning? What about your vision?"

"My ribs and chest hurt. My eyes . . . I don't know. I guess you could say it's cloudy when I look at things."

"Would you say it's a bad day or an average day?"

"You sound like those fool doctors and nurses: asking on a scale of one to ten how I feel. How can they know anything about how I feel when their idea of ten may not be the same as my idea of ten?"

"I'm just trying to have some way of gauging if the pot is working."

"I'll tell you if it's working."

Kate smiled through her gritted teeth. "Okay. Well, I'm going to take my shower." The phone rang just as Kate was leaving the kitchen. "Hello. Oh, hi Charlotte. Seriously? Uh, okay. Can you come in about half an hour? I was just about to shower. Okay, thanks. See you then." Kate hung up the phone and looked at Ruby. "Charlotte is coming over with two offers on the house, and they are both for more than I'm asking."

"Congratulations," Ruby said without much conviction, the fear and anxiety apparent on her face,

"Well, that doesn't mean they are good offers. They might include a whole bunch of contingencies or something. And it takes time to go through escrow and everything. Nothing's going to happen for a couple of months I shouldn't think." Ruby said nothing. "I'll just go shower now." Kate hurried out. She needed to think and she didn't want Ruby's stony silence to cloud it.

33

CHARLOTTE ARRIVED IN A FLURRY OF EXCITEMENT AND FRENZY. Ruby reacted by going to her room and slamming the door. "These are both good offers, Kate! One is for a little more than asking price and it's all cash. The other one is a couple of thousand more, but bank financing." She put the papers on the kitchen table and sat down. She started rummaging through her purse for a pen. "It's up to you, but my advice would be to take the all cash offer. They're ready to move in as soon as possible, and you won't have to wait for the bank's approval."

"Hold on, Charlotte. Let me look at the papers. Is there some rush?"

"You have twenty-four hours and I got the offers late last night. By the way, they both commented on how beautiful the back yard was."

Kate smiled. "I'll have to tell Ruby. Well, can you give me a couple of hours to read through this and think about what I want to do?"

Charlotte was about to answer when her cellphone rang. "Excuse me for a minute, Kate. Hello?" She covered the mouthpiece and turned to Kate, "Another offer!"

Things were moving so fast. Kate hadn't expected to be making all these decisions right away. It wasn't about the price; it was about how soon she could move out. She wasn't concerned about herself. She could always stay with Julia or Lucy for a couple of weeks if the closing didn't coincide with her Peace Corps start date. But was Ruby ready for this? And was Lawrence? And she still hadn't figured out what to do about Crosby. She knew Jessica would love to have him, but she had never spoken to Mike to see if it was okay with him.

Charlotte hung up and leaned back in her chair, laughing. "You have quite the hot piece of property. Maybe you should wait and see. This offer is for more than both of the other two."

"Can I just wait or do I have to respond to all the offers?"

"Well if you don't respond it's obvious that you rejected them, but it's always best to respond just to be polite and not turn anyone off."

"I need some time, Charlotte." Kate stood. "I'll call you in a couple of hours."

Actually, Kate was anxious to see how Ruby was doing, and whether she was feeling anything from the cookie. "That's fine. I'll go back to my office and let you know about the new offer after I get the fax. At least you can know what it's for when you make your decision." Charlotte left and Kate went immediately to Ruby's door and knocked.

"Ruby? She's gone. Can I come in?"

"Yes."

Kate entered and saw Ruby lying on her bed, petting Crosby. "Feel anything yet?"

"No."

Kate looked at the clock. "It hasn't been an hour yet. Charlotte is gone for now. Do you want to stay in here or come out to the kitchen?"

"I'll be out in a minute."

Kate left and sat down to inspect the real estate papers, but she had a hard time focusing on them. Her mind was actually on Lawrence. It was times like this that she wished she had someone to discuss things with, someone whose opinion she totally trusted. As good friends as she was with Julia and Lucy, and as much as she admired and respected her father, it was Lawrence she wanted to ask. Yep. That John Lennon quote always seems to be appropriate to every situation: "Life is what happens when you're busy making other plans."

34

KATE SCANNED THE TWO OFFERS AS SHE WAITED FOR RUBY TO JOIN HER IN THE KITCHEN. After a half hour had passed, and after Charlotte had called with the terms of the other offer, she went back to Ruby's bedroom and knocked. "Just checking on you. How are you feeling?"

"The same."

"It's been almost an hour and a half. Maybe you should take a little more."

"Okay."

"Do you want me to bring it in or will you come out here?"

"Bring it here with some more coffee."

Kate was about to open the door to get Ruby's coffee cup, but decided she would just bring in another one. She went back to the kitchen and broke off another small piece of the cookie. She brought it to her nose and made a face. "Yuck." She was surprised that Ruby was willing to eat it, but figured when you're in pain, and your eyesight is going, you are probably willing to try anything. She brought the coffee and cookie in to Ruby and sat down on the bed.

"So you don't feel anything? Not even a buzz?"

Ruby shrugged. "Maybe a little, but the pain isn't any better."

"How about the eyesight?"

"Hard to tell."

"Why don't you come out to the living room and watch some television. Then you'll be able to tell if it's working on the glaucoma."

Ruby sighed. "I don't know."

The phone rang and Kate went to the kitchen to answer it. "Hello? This morning? You know, there are three offers on the house already? Yes. I know you can keep showing it if there are offers. But this morning's not a good time. Maybe you could come later today. Okay. Two o'clock. Bye." She shouted to Ruby, "I just want to let you know that someone is showing the house this afternoon." Ruby didn't answer, but Kate hadn't expected her to. She knew that Ruby was anxious and frightened by this whole thing. So much had happened to her. So much had happened to both of them.

The offers were all good. Kate had to admit it felt good to own a house that was so sought after, but she knew that much of it had to do with Ruby's magical green thumb in the back yard. The location helped, but the presentation was what did it. She decided to wait for Charlotte to bring the third offer over, and if there were no contingencies and it was all cash, she would accept that one, even if they wanted to close escrow sooner rather than later. She was ready to go. She would have time to pack and put things in storage. Ruby was well enough to travel to Los Angeles, and then she would be in good hands. She was sure Jessica's father would be happy to take Crosby into their home. There weren't that many loose ends after all.

She was about to call Lawrence when she looked up and saw Ruby standing in the doorway of the kitchen. "What's for lunch?"

"What would you like? I'm happy to make it for you."

"Doesn't matter. I'm just very hungry."

"I can make you some soup or eggs."

"Either. Crosby and I will be in the living room." Ruby picked up Crosby and spoke baby talk to him, kissing and petting him as she left. Kate could hear giggling in the living room as she made the lunch.

Kate brought Ruby an omelet and toast and set it down on the coffee table. "So, I guess it's working?"

"Well, sort of. I feel better, but it takes so long."

"That's what Julia said would happen with the cookies. Would you like to try that vaporizer?"

"No. I don't know. Maybe."

Kate watched Ruby, marveling at the fact that the whole omelet vanished. That was definitely a first. "Can you see the television better? Do you want to try knitting and see if it helps for that?"

Ruby glared at Kate. "Could you just let me eat? Always so many questions!"

Kate slinked away. Just when she thought their relationship was becoming easy and comfortable, Ruby would throw her a zinger. Kate's mother had died when she was a baby, but she imagined this was typical of most mother/daughter relationships. At least this was the way she observed her friends' dealings with both their mothers and their daughters. She would call Lawrence and tell him the latest developments. That made her smile.

35

KATE AVOIDED RESPONDING TO THE OFFERS UNTIL AFTER THE TWO PM GROUP HAD LEFT. They seemed interested even after the realtor told them that there were already three offers. Ruby stayed in the living room, refusing to budge, and barely acknowledging the people when they said hello. Kate kept herself busy in the back yard, pretending to garden. Actually, though, she was just trying to be alone so she could make some decisions. She had spoken to Lawrence, and he had been very supportive of her waiting for the best offer, but she wasn't sure if that was entirely unselfish. Not that he was balking at taking Ruby to his home, but rather that he didn't want to see Kate go to Africa. Maybe that was wishful thinking on Kate's part, but she was pretty sure that he felt the same way she did. She was also ambivalent at this point, but she was trying not to let that cloud her judgment. She would discuss it with Charlotte who was planning to be over shortly.

She checked on Ruby and was about to ask her if she wanted or needed another piece of the cookie, but decided to wait to be asked. Anyway, Ruby had fallen asleep in front of the television. Charlotte arrived with the latest offer and said that the realtor who had just been there to show the house, had called to say an offer from these people was imminent. "You are probably wise to wait, although that would not normally be my advice."

"It's not about the money, per se."

"Then why are you waiting?"

"I just didn't expect this to happen so soon. Maybe I'm not mentally ready."

"Well, some people are never ready to sell. The house is filled with memories and—"

"No. It's not that," Kate interrupted. She glanced toward the living room.

At that moment, Charlotte noticed the bag of cookies sitting on the table and smiled. "I've been using pot for years for my back."

"Oh?" Kate was about to interject that it was for Ruby, but stopped herself. She didn't need to be defensive and she certainly didn't need to put Ruby in an awkward position. "Does it work well?"

"Sometimes. Often enough that I use it pretty regularly."

"Do you smoke it?"

"Sometimes, but I prefer to eat it."

"Really? How much do you take, if you don't mind me asking?"

"It depends. After a while you figure out how much. It also depends on the particular thing you're eating. They are all different. Are you just starting to use it?"

Kate wasn't sure how to answer. "Yes. We are." There. That was a fair response.

Charlotte reached in her purse and brought out a pouch. "I carry my doctor referral with me in case I get stopped and questioned, but I have a friend who gets me some really good stuff."

"You don't use the delivery service then either?"

"I don't know anyone who uses them anymore. It's too expensive, and the stuff you get underground is better, in my opinion." She reached into the pouch and took out what looked like a piece of peanut brittle. "Try this. It tastes way better than any cookies or brownies I've had. And smell it."

Kate did. "Doesn't smell bad at all."

"Taste it."

"Not now." Kate smiled. "I need to stay focused to read these offers."

Charlotte broke off a piece and handed it to her. "Try it later and let me know. I can get you plenty more if you want."

"Okay. Thanks."

"Well, let's get to work. Have you read through the two offers from yesterday?"

"Yes."

"And?"

"I was thinking of maybe waiting to see all the offers, but I don't know. Maybe I should just accept one of these and get it over with."

"It's up to you."

"I guess I should go with the all cash one, even though it's not the highest price."

"That's what I'd do if you want to make the whole process faster and easier. When did they say they wanted to close?"

"Thirty days. But, maybe I need more time than that. I need to contact my Peace Corps representative."

"Then we can counter with the change of closing date."

Kate breathed a sigh of relief. "I guess I have backups if they balk at changing the date."

Charlotte laughed. "Yes. You do have reserves up the yin yang!"

"Well, let's just go ahead. I don't want to think about it anymore." Kate was anxious to get Charlotte out so she could give Ruby the peanut brittle. She wanted to see if this worked better and faster. "Why don't you fill out the paperwork in your office, and I'll stop by and sign there."

"You can sign now, and I'll fill it out. You want to accept the offer as is except for the closing date. Correct?" Kate shook her head. "What date should I write down? Do you need to talk to someone first?"

"I guess I need to call the Peace Corps. I'll just sign the papers and then I'll call you with the date."

Charlotte took the forms out of her bag and showed Kate where to sign. When that was done, Charlotte gathered the papers and stuffed them back in her bag. She started to put the pouch back in her bag, but then left it on the table. "You keep this and let me know if you want more." She winked at Kate and left.

Kate peeked into the living room and saw that Ruby was awake. She went in and sat down. "I accepted an offer on the house but I haven't set a closing date. I wanted to talk to you first."

"I heard you. I thought you had to talk to the Peace Corps to find out."

"That was a lie. I already know the date for that. It's actually next month."

"Then why did you say thirty days was too soon?"

"I don't know. I . . . um . . . just did."

Ruby shook her head. "You're crazy sometimes."

Kate laughed. "Yes, I suppose."

"I need to talk to Lawrence, then."

"I already did." Ruby looked a little surprised and maybe a tad angry, but said nothing. "He's very happy to have you come anytime. He did say that you might be more comfortable at Michael's house. Lawrence lives in a high-rise condo in Westwood. Michael and Carla live in a house in the valley. They have a yard and plenty of room. And Danielle would be very excited for you to be there. Lawrence said he would come by to visit a lot."

Ruby shrugged. "Okay."

Kate was a little disappointed at Ruby's reaction. She had hoped that Ruby would act more excited about going there. But then she remembered that Ruby was not exactly the most effusive person. "And there's something else I want to talk to you about."

Ruby sighed. "What else?"

Kate felt her cheeks get hot at the typical Ruby response. But she let it go and went on. "Charlotte uses marijuana also, for her back pain. She left me some peanut brittle for you to try."

"You telling everyone my business?"

"No. I didn't say it was for you. She saw the bag of cookies, and I just let her assume it was for me." Kate went on. "She said that the peanut brittle works fast and stays with you longer. She can get us more if it works better than the cookies."

"And how would I get it when I'm at Lawrence's. Oh, excuse me, Michael's. I forgot that everyone else is deciding what's best for me."

"Oh Ruby! We are all just trying to help. Why can't you accept that?"

Ruby looked away. Luckily Crosby came over and jumped onto Ruby's lap to diffuse the situation. Kate knew Ruby never said she was sorry. Silence and then moving on was the closest she ever came to apologizing. "So where's this peanut brittle?"

Kate went to the kitchen and brought the pouch back with her. "I'm not sure how much, but if it's more potent than the cookies, I guess we should start with a small piece."

"Just break off some and give it to me."

Kate happily gave her a small piece. "If this works well, I'll talk to Lawrence and Charlotte and see if we can work something out."

"So Lawrence and Charlotte will be my drug dealers?"

Kate sighed. "Maybe there's a place in Los Angeles to buy it legally. It's a big city and they have dispensaries there. And you'll have an address there. I'm sure there's a way to figure it out."

"Maybe I can learn how to make it, myself."

"Yes!" Kate was thrilled. "That's a great idea. Just make sure to keep it away from Danielle!"

Ruby's face immediately went ashen. "Oh dear. I hadn't thought of that."

"Just make sure to keep it in a safe place in your room. I need to call Lawrence to talk about a date for you to move there. And then Charlotte."

"If it's okay with them, I'm ready to go. You can keep the thirty days."

"I'll call now." She started to go to the kitchen. "Unless you want to talk to Lawrence yourself?"

"No. You make the arrangements."

"I can bring you down, but it's a long car ride, probably seven hours. We could fly, if you'd rather?"

Ruby's face tightened. "I don't know."

"Have you ever flown?"

"Not much and not for many years."

"It's a pretty quick trip. It's a little more than an hour from San Francisco." Kate realized at that moment that Ruby's whole demeanor had changed. She seemed more alert and she was smiling. Something she didn't do often. "Are you feeling effects from the peanut brittle?"

"Why yes. I feel better."

Kate wanted to high-five her, but just smiled. "That's wonderful."

Ruby stood, with nowhere near as much effort as it usually took. "I think I'll look for something to eat."

"Great. And I'll go call Lawrence."

Kate watched Ruby walk out without her usual discomfort and wincing. She thought that perhaps things were actually turning around for everyone. She started to daydream about the one big happy family that this group had become. Maybe the marijuana was the medicine that would give Ruby several more good years. Maybe Kate and Lawrence could get together after she got home. Maybe she'd move back to Venice and she and Lawrence could buy a house there together. Her brain could go in a million directions when she gave it permission.

36

KATE ACCEPTED THE OFFER AS IT WAS WRITTEN, AND BOTH BUYER AND SELLER SIGNED THE CONTRACT. Things moved very quickly from then on. She made plane reservations to bring Ruby to Los Angeles. Michael and Carla started to prepare their spare bedroom, and Charlotte had promised to send Ruby off with a good amount of peanut brittle, enough to last her until she found a source in Los Angeles. Ruby had acquiesced to letting Charlotte know it was for her, and Charlotte was more than happy to keep her supplied. After all, she had made a bundle on Kate's house very quickly and easily. It was the least she could do. Kate was a little wary about getting on the plane with it, since they didn't have a medical referral, but she figured no one would suspect an old woman who could barely walk. She would hide it in Ruby's knitting bag.

Kate and Lawrence spoke every day and he always made sure to talk to Ruby for a few minutes, as well. Everyone seemed quite at ease with each other in their newly acquired family. Carla also called several times to ask how Ruby would like her room decorated and what she liked to eat. A week ago Kate would have told her just to keep a good supply of coffee and toast on hand, but now Ruby was eating much more heartily. It wasn't unusual for her to eat three genuine meals a day, not to mention having the munchies in between.

Ruby's pain and eyesight had improved, but Kate thought she should have her heart checked before leaving for Los Angeles. "How about getting an EKG?"

Ruby balked. "If I'm not going to do anything about it, what's the point? I don't need to know."

"Okay. I get that. But you need to find a doctor when you're down there, and it would be good to bring him results so he'll know what's going on."

"Who says I'm getting a doctor? Listen to me. I may die tomorrow or live for another twenty years. No doctor can tell me when it's going to happen and they can't change it."

Kate had to agree. "Okay. Whatever you wish. But there's something else I've been meaning to ask you. What about your things that are still in Mississippi? I mean, don't you want them?"

Ruby looked out the window and said nothing. After several minutes, Kate decided to continue her own packing. Ruby either hadn't thought about it or hadn't decided what to do about it. Or perhaps, she had already taken care of things back in Mississippi without sharing any of that information with Kate. After all, Kate sometimes forgot that Ruby had lived for many years without Kate's micromanaging.

Kate got a definite date from the Peace Corps. Her training and orientation would start three days after escrow closed on her house. She figured she could stay with Julia or Lucy for those two nights. She spoke with her neighbor, Mike, who said Crosby could live with them for the two years that Kate would be in Africa. Although it was a relief to know that Crosby would have a good home, she also knew that Jessica was a teenager, and that other things might take precedence. Mike was merely being accommodating. It was Jessica who would be doing the caretaking, so Kate did feel slightly uneasy about it.

Ruby seemed happy about going to Los Angeles. Or maybe she was just happy from the peanut brittle. No matter. She was pleasant and even funny. Julia and Lucy took them out to dinner to say goodbye. They had suggested a place that specialized in ribs and southern cooking. Kate had expected Ruby to grouse about how it wasn't the same food that they had in Mississippi, but instead she ate with more gusto than Kate had ever seen.

The evening before Ruby and Kate were to get on the plane, they were in the living room with the television droning. Crosby was snoring on Ruby's lap. Ruby's sight was good enough for her to knit and Kate was still attempting it. She thought she'd have nights in Africa when she would want something to do with her time, figuring Internet service and television might not be an option. Of course, she was also aware that wool scarves would probably not be necessary in Africa, but she didn't care if she actually finished any item. She would just take one skein of yarn and unravel the finished product and start over. Anyway, she wouldn't have that much room in her suitcase for a lot of skeins. The phone rang, and Kate went into the kitchen to answer it. "Hello? Well, hi Danielle. Ruby is really looking forward to seeing you tomorrow and I am too. Okay. Just a minute, I'll bring her the phone." Kate took the receiver into the living room. "Danielle wants to talk to you."

Ruby smiled and took the phone. "Hello, sugar." Ruby furrowed her brow and glanced at Kate. "Well, I don't know. I'll have to ask her."

"Ask me what?" Kate looked at Ruby inquisitively.

"Danielle wants to know if I could bring Crosby to live with us."

Kate grinned. "Is that okay with Carla and Michael?"

"Kate wants to know if it's okay with your parents. Oh hi Carla." Ruby turned toward Kate. "Yes."

Kate was ecstatic! "That's wonderful! I wonder how you bring a cat on a plane. I'll have to call the airline."

Ruby talked a few more minutes with Carla and then handed the receiver to Kate. "She wants to talk to you."

"Hello? Yes. I'm thrilled. I was going to leave him with my neighbor, but I wasn't sure it was the best thing. This is perfect. He loves Ruby. Okay. See you tomorrow." She hung up and took the receiver back to the kitchen to call the airlines. She remembered how Jed had left his cat, Mother, with her Dad in Venice and then got her back years later. She smiled. Things always do seem to work out. There is another more positive way of looking at that John Lennon quote. Good things can happen in life even when your plans don't seem to be the best ones.

37

NEITHER KATE NOR RUBY SLEPT VERY WELL THAT NIGHT. Kate had kept Crosby in her room instead of letting him sleep with Ruby, which was his usual nighttime habit. Kate wanted one more night with her cat, but Crosby spent most of it clawing at the door and meowing. Kate finally relented and let him out. It was already three a.m., so even if Kate had fallen asleep right away, she would have gotten only a couple of hours sleep.

The plane left at eleven, but the drive to the airport was at least an hour and a half without traffic, and they had to be even earlier than the customary one hour because of Crosby. He could go in the cabin with them, but he had to go in a carrier that fit under the seat in front, just like any carry-on bag. Kate had decided to buy the one that the airline provided. She had no idea how Crosby would react to the whole process and figured the one that the airline provided would be sturdy and also fit under the seat. Kate didn't need anything else to worry about. She had enough on her plate at the moment.

She finally got out of bed at six, giving up on any possibility of more sleep. When she stumbled into the kitchen to put the coffee on, she found Ruby sitting at the kitchen table. "Wow. You're already up?"

"Couldn't sleep."

"Me neither." Kate decided not to add that it was mostly because of Crosby. "Breakfast or just coffee?"

"Neither. I'm not hungry."

"Did you have any peanut brittle this morning?"

"No. I think I'll wait."

"It might calm you for the flight."

"Well, I'd rather feel more in control."

"If that's what you wish."

"Well, what will I do when I get there?"

"I've already spoken to Lawrence about it. He said he'll find something for you, even if it's not peanut brittle."

"Hmm."

"I'm sure it will be okay and he'll find you something you'll like."

"But it's not, you know . . ."

"Legal?"

Ruby nodded. "Yes."

"Don't worry about that. He's a smart man. He's a professor with a PhD. He'll figure something out. Maybe you can get the referral when you're down there."

Ruby took a breath and got up slowly. "Maybe I'll go have a bite of peanut brittle after all." She walked slowly out of the room.

They arrived at the airport with plenty of time. Kate would only stay one night, so she just had a small backpack. Ruby never did have much with her as she had only originally planned to be in San Francisco for a few days. Goodness, that was so long ago. She had managed with what she originally brought from Mississippi with Kate buying her just a few more items of clothing and skeins of yarn. So besides her suitcase and knitting bag, she only had Martin's guitar. Kate bought the carrier for Crosby and with a great deal of resistance on his part, she was finally able to get him inside. He clawed and meowed loudly all the way to the gate. The vet said not to give him a sedative or tranquilizer, so the trip was probably going to be a bit noisy for the passengers in the cabin. At least the trip was only a little more than an hour.

The trip was uneventful, although Ruby spent the entire hour clutching her knitting needles without taking a stitch. Kate started out trying to quiet Crosby, but she wasn't allowed to remove him from the carrier so she gave up after a while. The cat, however, did not give up. She just hoped that she was seated amidst understanding cat lovers. Ruby finally exhaled when the tires hit the ground in Los Angeles and put her needles away. The whole cabin probably breathed a sigh of relief as well, tired of listening to Crosby.

Lawrence, Michael, Carla and Danielle were all waiting at the bottom of the escalator near the baggage claim. Danielle ran up to Ruby and hugged her legs. Michael and Carla hugged Kate and took the cat carrier and guitar. Lawrence took Kate's hand and walked with her to the baggage carousel. At first, Kate stiffened, not sure she was ready for Ruby to see what Lawrence's and her relationship had become. But she relaxed quickly as her heart melted from Lawrence's touch, and she didn't care one iota about Ruby's reaction.

38

AFTER DINNER THAT EVENING, THEY ALL RELAXED IN THE LIVING ROOM WITH COFFEE AND DESSERT. Crosby did not have any residual trauma from his plane ride and had settled into his new home. It certainly helped that Danielle was feeding him and holding him continually since they had arrived. The conversation never let up either, as there was much catching up to do on everyone's part. Danielle got tired of playing with Crosby and interrupted the group. "Grandma Ruby?"

"Yes sugar?"

"Will you play the guitar for me?"

Kate looked at Ruby expectantly. Would she do it? She had never played for Kate and as far as she knew, hadn't picked it up at all since Joel had dropped it off. Danielle would be the only one she would play for, but would she play in front of everyone? Once again, Ruby surprised Kate. "Go get it for me, honey. I'll see what I can remember."

Danielle ran into Ruby's room to get the guitar, and Kate looked at Lawrence in disbelief.

But Lawrence hadn't spent any part of the last sixty years with his mother and didn't know that this was so out of character. Instead, he smiled broadly, happy to discover another side to her. "What kind of music do you play, Ruby?" Carla asked.

"I can do country, jazz, pop, but mostly blues. I used to play in a band." She took a deep breath and turned to Lawrence. "That's how I met your father."

You could have cut the silence with a knife. No one was sure what to say. Lawrence finally spoke. "Now, that's pretty cool. Both my parents were musicians."

Everyone breathed a sigh of relief, and the tension was broken just as Danielle entered dragging the guitar case behind her. "Here Grandma Ruby."

"Oh my. That guitar is bigger than you are!" Ruby took the guitar case and opened it. Everyone was quiet as she tuned it. "Bring me a towel, Danielle, so I can wipe off the dust."

Danielle ran to the kitchen and returned with a towel. Still everyone waited silently for Ruby to begin playing. And when she did, they all gasped. Her talent as a guitarist was obvious. It may have been a long time since she played, but she was still able to remember some difficult and amazing riffs. Danielle was mesmerized, and when Ruby finished and everyone had finished clapping, she asked, "Will you teach me?"

"Of course, sugar, but I think you may need to start with a smaller guitar."

"I think that can be arranged, " Michael answered.

"Do you sing too?" Carla asked.

Ruby began to play and sing "Careless Love," and again the result was awe-inspiring. She played a couple more songs and then put down the guitar. "I think I'll have to brush up on my repertoire."

Kate was shocked at how comfortable and relaxed Ruby was in this new environment. It had taken so long for her to be at ease in Kate's house. Kate smiled as she glanced around the room. Lawrence saw her smile and squeezed her hand. He probably didn't realize exactly what she was smiling at, but it didn't matter. There was a lot to smile about tonight. But then she remembered that she was leaving tomorrow to go home, and then a few days later to go to Africa. There were also reasons not to smile.

Danielle had climbed onto her mother's lap and leaned into her sleepily. Ruby and Crosby had both been yawning for the last several minutes. Kate and Lawrence looked at each other and nodded. It was time to go.

"It's getting late," said Kate.

"Where are you sleeping?" Ruby asked.

"The sofa here is very comfortable, and you're certainly welcome to stay here," Michael replied. Carla started to speak but then glanced at Kate who looked at Lawrence, expectantly.

"She'll stay at my apartment. It's closer to the airport," Lawrence added quickly.

"That makes sense, then." Kate spoke before anyone could protest. She turned to Michael and Carla. "It has been wonderful spending time with you and getting to know you." They hugged. "And you take good care of Ruby for me, Danielle."

"I will. I promise," Danielle said and gave Kate a hug.

Then Kate turned to Ruby. "Well, I'll be back in two years. I'll write often, and maybe we can Skype if I can find a good Internet cafe in Johannesburg."

"Skype?" Ruby asked.

"Carla and Michael can show you. It's a way to talk to each other on computer in real time, looking at each other."

"Oh Lawdy! Not another thing I gotta learn!"

They all laughed. "You are becoming a tech wizard, Ruby."

"Never thought I'd . . ." Ruby stopped talking and looked at Kate.

Kate wiped away the tear that was rolling down her cheek. She took Ruby's hand. It had been an impulsive movement. If she had thought about it, she probably would have thought Ruby wouldn't have taken it and Kate would have been embarrassed, humiliated and angry. But she would have been wrong. Ruby took the hand and pulled Kate close to her.

They stood, embracing, for several minutes. Carla picked up Danielle and took her to bed. Michael and Lawrence stood and waited awkwardly, not sure if they should leave or stay. Finally, Ruby and Kate unlocked their arms and looked into each other's faces, both of them wet with tears.

"Thanks for teaching me how to knit and helping me with my garden."

"Thanks for teaching me how to Google." Ruby giggled as she said it and Kate smiled. "And thanks for taking care of me," Ruby finally said.

Kate couldn't believe her ears. Did she hear that right? Ruby finally acknowledged it? "I forgive you," Kate blurted out before she had time to think about whether or not it was wise to bring all that up.

Ruby took a deep breath. "I'm sorry I treated you poorly all those years ago."

Kate took Ruby's hand and held it. "Thank you for saying that. It means a lot to me. I only wish Martin could have had this opportunity too."

Ruby didn't answer and turned to go to her room. As she walked away she said, "I'll take good care of Crosby."

"I know you will." Kate called after her. She turned to Lawrence and took his arm. "Are you ready?"

"At your service."

"Good luck," Michael called after them.

There wasn't much conversation in the car going to Lawrence's. He felt that she probably wanted to be alone with her thoughts, and he was right. Her mind raced in a million directions, but it came down to one pervasive feeling of sadness for what she had lost once, and what she would lose now.

They entered Lawrence's apartment hand in hand. It was sparsely but tastefully furnished in teak and glass, without knickknacks or decorative wall hangings. There were some framed nature photographs on the walls, family photos on one table, a couple of oriental rugs covering some of the polished wood floors, and track lighting rather than lamps. "It looks like a bachelor lives here. It's nice. I like it."

"I'm not here that much, actually. I'm either at work, at the gym, or at Michael's."

"No hobbies?"

"I took those photographs on the walls. That's how I spend the rest of my time: hiking or driving, looking for the perfect shot."

"Have you traveled much?"

"Not much internationally, just the usual tourist traps in Europe and Mexico, and not in recent years. My wife and I traveled some in the early days of our marriage."

"These are beautiful photos. You are very talented."

"Maybe with retirement looming, I'll be able to get more into it. And maybe more traveling too."

"Maybe you'd like to visit South Africa sometime." Kate smiled.

"Lawrence nodded and winked. "Maybe sooner than you think." He took her in his arms. "Shall I show you the guest room?"

"I think I'd prefer to see your room." They walked into his bedroom with their arms still around each other.

39

THE MORNING ARRIVED MUCH TOO QUICKLY. Kate didn't want to leave for more than just the obvious reason: Lawrence. She was also dreading the final packing and cleanup of her house, as well as the chores associated with leaving the country for two years. And then there were all the goodbyes, something she was not good at and usually shirked by leaving places quickly and quietly. Not that she hadn't thought about doing that, but she knew that Julia and Lucy would never allow it, and they had already told her that they were having a goodbye party for her whether she liked it or not.

She lay on the bed thinking about all this while she waited for Lawrence to wake up. She watched him sleep and couldn't help but think of Martin and the mornings they had spent in bed together. She was thankful that they didn't look anything alike. That would have been too weird, as if this wasn't weird enough. She peeked at the clock by Lawrence's side of the bed. It was almost seven and her plane left at eleven. She wanted to wake him so they could have more than a rushed ride to the airport, but their lovemaking had lasted into the wee hours of the morning, and he probably needed his sleep. After all, he was still working; he didn't have the luxury of taking naps whenever he felt like it, as she did. Well, she didn't have to ponder on it for long, because he opened his eyes, smiled, and pulled her to him.

As it turned out, by the time they got out of bed, it was a rushed ride to the airport. But that probably made the whole thing easier to handle. They could feel anxiety about getting to the airport on time, instead of about saying goodbye. Lawrence pulled up to the terminal and in order to make her flight, Kate had no choice but to give him a cursory kiss and a promise to call when she got home.

The next few days were spent running errands, cleaning house, and saying goodbyes. She and Lawrence texted and called throughout the days, and she and Ruby spoke often as well. Before she knew it, it was the night before she was supposed to leave for Africa. She had sold her car, and the man who bought it had been nice enough to let her use it until this afternoon. The people who had bought her house were also nice enough to let her sleep in a sleeping bag on the floor this last night, even though, technically, the house was theirs. The closing had been that afternoon as well. Julia and Lucy were going to pick her up early the next morning to drive her to the airport. She was packed and ready to go, and had settled into her sleeping bag with half a bottle of wine and her cell phone. She wanted her last conversation with Lawrence to be warm and cozy. He had promised to call when he got home from a meeting at the university.

She played solitaire on her phone while waiting for his call. It finally came after ten, later than he had expected it to be.

"Kate?" His voice sounded strange: distant and cracking.

"What is it Lawrence? Was the meeting that bad?"

"Kate . . . I . . ."

"Lawrence! What's going on?"

He exhaled loudly into the phone. "It's Ruby."

"What happened?"

"Heart attack . . . tonight . . ."

"Oh no! Is she in the hospital?"

"No, Kate. She . . . didn't make it."

At first, she couldn't speak or even breathe. She finally gasped, and the tears started to flow. "What?"

"I debated about telling you now. I thought maybe I should wait until you had already left. But I thought you'd be furious if I'd done that."

"Yes. I would have been. Lawrence, let me call you back in a couple of minutes. I need to catch my breath and —"

"I understand," Lawrence interrupted. "Call me back when you can."

Kate hung up the phone and got out of her sleeping bag. She paced around the house, taking swigs of her wine bottle and sobbing loudly, letting out months, maybe even years, of emotions. After several minutes, she sat on the floor of what had been Ruby's room and called Lawrence back. "I will be on a plane to Los Angeles in the morning. I'll make the arrangements and let you know what time it gets in. No. You'll be busy. I'll rent a car."

"Kate! You don't have to do this."

"Yes, I do. I will call the Peace Corps office first thing in the morning and tell them what happened. I can postpone my arrival until after the funeral. What are they going to do? Fire me?"

"Well, you don't have to rent a car. Let me know what time your plane gets in and I'll be there."

"Okay. I would like that better. Well, I have to call Julia and Lucy before it gets too late and let them know what's going on . . . and the airlines . . . and maybe there's an emergency number for the Peace Corps office . . . I'm sorry, just thinking aloud. I'll let you know when the flight gets in."

"Okay. I need to get over to Carla and Michael's."

"Did she die quickly?"

"She had gone to bed early. She said she wasn't feeling well, and Carla went to check on her about nine o'clock."

"I hope it was quick and painless and in her sleep."

"Yes. Let's just assume it was."

"Good idea."

"Kate?"

"Yes?"

"I love you."

It had been many years since anyone had said that to her. She was somewhat taken aback and not sure how to respond. She felt the same way, but wasn't sure if she was ready to say it. She took a deep breath and answered, "I love you too, Lawrence."

40

KATE'S PLANE TOUCHED DOWN AT NINE-THIRTY. Lawrence was waiting at the gate. He had managed to talk his way through security by using his mother's death as an emergency reason to be there. Kate was on the phone most of the night, either leaving messages or waking people up. By the time she sat down on the plane, she was physically and emotionally exhausted and had fallen asleep before takeoff.

She woke up just as the plane landed and she thought that she must look like hell. She figured she'd have time to go to the ladies room before seeing Lawrence. But when she saw him standing at the gate, it didn't much matter anymore what she looked like. She fell into his arms and allowed the tears to come. They may have been tears of exhaustion mixed in with the grief, but she was surprised at how she let herself go in the security of his embrace.

They stood holding on to each other, without speaking, for several minutes. Finally Lawrence asked, "Did you check any luggage?"

"No. I just grabbed the suitcase and backpack I was taking to Africa."

"What did you tell the Peace Corps?"

"I could only leave messages. I told them there had been a death in the family, and that I wouldn't be on the scheduled flight and to please call me." She took her phone out of the pocket of her jeans and looked at it. "I forgot to switch it out of airplane mode, but there are no calls yet."

"I'm glad you got a flight to Burbank. It's so much easier to get in and out of."

"Further from your house, though."

"Just by eight miles and ten minutes."

"One would think you were a professor of Mathematics instead of English."

Lawrence smiled. "Have you forgotten what it's like living in Los Angeles? You live your life by how long it takes to drive places."

"I guess I had forgotten that lifestyle. How's Danielle taking Ruby's death?"

Lawrence shook his head. "She's very distraught. She and Ruby had become so close. Did you know they slept together?"

"How did Crosby take that?"

"Oh, he just joined in. It was the three of them."

Kate smiled, imagining the love fest that must have been. "Carla was okay with that? I mean I'd be worried that Danielle wouldn't be getting enough sleep or something."

"Carla was thrilled that Danielle finally had a Grandma." He took a breath. "Although only for a short time."

Kate clutched Lawrence's hand and squeezed it. "Interesting how we've all had the same lack of family growing up."

"It's probably not that unusual. We are brought up believing that everyone is part of some large, warm, loving extended family and we are somehow the misfits. I don't think it's true. And anyway, the problem is only that society makes us think that it's the only way or the right way . . . we know plenty of people who have managed just fine without it."

"And there are those who have it and are not managing well at all."

They arrived at Lawrence's car. "Do you want to go to my house first and drop off your things?"

"Yes. Is that okay?"

"There's a lot to do, but no hurry to get it done, other than to get you on your way to Africa." He looked into her eyes. "And the rest of your life." She looked back at him, not quite sure what he meant by that. "Your words, not mine. Remember?"

"Yes, I guess so." They rode all the way back to Lawrence's apartment in silence, not uncomfortable, just pensive.

They still hadn't spoken when they got inside his living room, and he took her bags and put them in his bedroom. He came out and pulled her close to him. They kissed and walked back to the bedroom, still without any words. The lovemaking was tinged with a sense of desperation and urgency, but it was also soothing and fulfilling. When it was over, Kate fell asleep immediately, and Lawrence lay next to her, never taking his eyes off her face, occasionally touching her cheek with the back of his hand.

41

KATE OPENED HER EYES AND SAW LAWRENCE LOOKING DOWN ON HER. For a brief moment she was brought back to a life of many years ago when Martin would do the same thing. But it was different, because the look on Lawrence's face was pure pleasure and marvel, while Martin's had always been one of apprehension and regret. There was no denying it. Although they had not been identical twins and their skin color did not match, their facial features had an uncanny resemblance.

"Hi." Lawrence smiled and kissed her.

"Did you sleep?" she asked between kisses.

"A little. Mostly I watched you sleep."

"What time is it?"

He looked at the clock. "Almost one."

She sat upright. "Oh dear! Did you call Michael? Were they expecting us?"

"It's okay. No hurry. Michael went to work and Carla is dealing with Danielle."

Kate fell back into the bed. "Of course there's no rush. It's not like there are people to notify. We don't know anyone to call. Unless she finally opened up to you these past couple of weeks?"

Lawrence shook his head. "Not about the past. We only talked about the present and the future."

Kate sighed. "There wasn't much future for the two of you."

Lawrence's eyes filled and he pursed his lips tightly, trying to hold his emotions inside. He succeeded at keeping the tears from spilling, but his voice cracked when he spoke. "Not enough to make up for all we missed." He stood up and started to dress. "I'll go make us some lunch while you get ready."

"Okay." Kate wasn't as successful at keeping the tears from rolling down her cheeks. She wasn't sure, again, whether she was crying about Ruby or Lawrence. Or herself. But it was then that she decided to call her father in New York. She hadn't talked to him last night to tell him all that had happened. She hadn't seen him in almost a year and she didn't know how long it would be until she would see him. But Ruby's death made her realize the fragility of life. He was in his eighties now and although he was healthy and agile, traveling to Africa would not be easy for him, so she didn't expect him to visit her. She knew she would want to see Lawrence on her own time off. Maybe Finn could come to Los Angeles and then he could meet Lawrence and his family.

She looked at her phone and saw she had several voicemails. She assumed they were from the Peace Corps people. She decided to wait to listen to them. She tried to call her father but he didn't answer. She left a message saying she'd call him later and got dressed. "Mmmmm smells good," she said as she entered the kitchen.

"Blueberry wheat germ pancakes. Do you want syrup?"

"No thanks. I like them plain. Not a maple fan."

"I didn't think you would want the extra sugar."

"You know me that well already?"

"Unlike the rest of you, your eating habits aren't that hard to figure out."

She kissed him on the top of his head and sat down. "So have you, Michael, and Carla talked about what arrangements you want to make for a funeral or memorial service?"

"I don't see a point to one. She didn't know anyone else here. Carla had tried to get some personal information out of her about her life in Mississippi – friends, relatives, neighbors, but she was mum. We don't even know who to call back there."

"So what were you thinking then?"

"Cremation and then scatter her ashes. We don't know where to scatter them though. It's odd. I thought I might bring them back to Mississippi to scatter them but . . . "

Kate took his hand. "If I still owned the house we could bury her ashes in the beautiful backyard she planted for me. But it seems like it would be an awfully odd request to the new owners."

Lawrence laughed. "Yes. I don't think they'd be very amenable to it."

"Well, we could plan something at the scattering with blues music – maybe we could find some recordings she was on?"

Lawrence shrugged. "I don't know. Maybe."

Kate took that as a signal to let things alone. There must be a lot going through his mind right now. You find your mother after sixty years and then lose her before you get to know her very well. That's more than Kate could say about her own mother. "These are delicious, by the way."

"I can cook a few things well."

"You can do a lot of things well."

"You're sweet."

Kate laughed. "I've been called a lot of things but I don't get called 'sweet' very often."

"Well, I think you're sweet. So you still haven't heard back from the Peace Corps?"

"Oh, I left my phone in the bedroom. There were a few messages, but I didn't listen to them."

"Why not?"

"I guess I just wasn't ready to think about it. I'm sure they will want to know when I am planning to come and I don't know what to say."

"Well, you should probably call them and tell them that."

"Yeah, you're right. I'll go return the calls now and then we can go over to Michael's."

"Okay, I'll do the dishes."

Kate got up from the table and started to leave. "I should call Peter too, I guess."

"Do you think he'd want to come to our makeshift memorial service?"

"I doubt it. He didn't know her either. Ruby was quite a mysterious woman."

"My mother the enigma."

"Well, maybe we all are," Kate added as she left the kitchen.

42

MOST OF THE PHONE MESSAGES WERE FROM THE PEACE CORPS OFFICE. There were a couple from Julia and Lucy, but she needed to call the Peace Corps back first, even if she didn't know what to tell them. The scattering of the ashes could happen as soon as the crematorium released them. Certainly she could leave in three or four days. She picked up the phone and listened to the voicemails again, but all they said was to call back right away so they could make new arrangements. They totally understood and were happy to accommodate her. Yet, she couldn't bring herself to press the call back numbers.

"What did they say?" Lawrence asked as he entered the bedroom.

"I didn't call them yet."

"Why not?"

"I don't know exactly." She looked at him almost as if she was begging him to answer the question for her.

"Do you want me to phone them? I could say you were too distraught to call." He smiled, kind of joking, but not really.

"No. It's silly. I should call." She looked at the phone again and then handed it to him. "Or not."

He smiled and pressed the first call back number. "Do I need to call all these numbers on the voicemail list?"

"Just the first three. The others can wait."

"I'll just tell them that you will call them as soon as you have information to give them on departure dates. Okay with you?"

"Perfect." She got off the bed and went into the bathroom. She wanted to freshen up but really she just didn't want to be there when he made the calls. She was not used to having people do things for her and she felt like a fool. But more than embarrassed by her weakness and indecision, she thought she might cry again and didn't want Lawrence to see that. And she couldn't explain that either.

Lawrence was not in the bedroom when she finally came out of the bathroom. She saw him in the living room, staring out the window. He smiled at her when she entered. "Ready to go?"

"Yes. What did they say?"

"Exactly what you would expect. Please give you their condolences and call as soon as you can."

She exhaled and put her purse over her shoulder. "Shall we?" They left hand in hand.

The welcome from all the people in the house was warm and filled with more tears. Even Crosby greeted her, something she was afraid might not happen. Such crazy paranoia people have about their animals. She was happy, though, to see how much love and attention he was getting. And how he was so comforting for Danielle.

"She hadn't talked about pain. I thought she was doing better." Carla was distraught and guilt-ridden.

"She hardly ever complained about pain. It just wasn't her way. Please, Carla, don't feel responsible." Kate hugged her.

"She was old and sick. She had how many heart attacks in the last few months?" Michael asked Kate.

"Three, I think. Michael's right. It was just her time. Think about it, Carla. Ruby was able to end her life, spending it with the family she never knew she had. She was probably happier than she'd ever been."

Carla shook her head and pulled Danielle onto her lap and kissed her. "Do you want some coffee or tea or anything?"

"Not for me. Kate?" Lawrence asked.

"I'm fine. So when did the crematorium say the ashes would be ready?"

"Tomorrow," Michael answered. "Does anyone have any idea what the next step should be?"

They all looked at each other. None of them were religious people, but they thought Ruby might be, coming from the Deep South and all. The biggest problem was that no one really knew her well enough to put together a proper memorial. And it wasn't like they had pictures. All they knew was that she played the guitar and sang in a blues band. She liked gardening and knitting. She was stubborn, opinionated, racist, and homophobic: these were not things one said about someone in a eulogy. The silence was interrupted by Kate's phone ringing. She looked at it and saw it was from Peter. "It's Peter. He's the man who had taken care of calling Ruby and me after Martin died. I left him a message, telling him what happened. I should call him back."

She went into what had been Ruby's bedroom. She saw the knitting bag on a chair, the guitar leaning against the wall, her purse on the bed and the tears welled up . . . again. Kate was flabbergasted at how much crying she was doing for Ruby, a woman she barely knew, and a relationship that had been ninety percent rocky.

Kate thought about how hard it was to put grief in a neat little bag. It not only differs among people, but changes in each person for every loss. And of course, there is the fact that each loss brings up all the others one has experienced in a lifetime. Kate realized she was probably crying for Martin, her own mother, and who knows how many others.

She wiped the tears, took a deep breath, and pressed the button to return Peter's call. He answered right away. "Oh, Kate. After all that's happened between you two. I can't believe it."

"I know. And you don't even know the half of all that's happened." She proceeded to tell Peter everything. They shared their disbelief about Lawrence and his family. They had a good laugh over the glaucoma and medical marijuana story. She told him about how she had transformed her back yard and taught her how to knit. "And I had brought her here to Los Angeles to live with Lawrence's son and daughter-in-law. I was supposed to leave for the Peace Corps in Africa the very day she died."

"So, where are you now?"

"In Los Angeles." She debated about whether she should tell Peter of her relationship with Lawrence and quickly decided that of course she should.

"That's quite a story."

"Yes. I guess it is. Falling in love with your dead ex-husband's brother!" She laughed. "It feels good to laugh."

"Is there a funeral?"

"There's really no need for one. She didn't know anyone here except Lawrence's family. And she's being cremated. They were going to scatter the ashes somewhere. Actually they aren't sure what to do."

"Well, what did she like? Gardening? Knitting? The Blues?"

"Yes. But that doesn't help in thinking of where to scatter her ashes. And no one is interested in traveling back to Mississippi to do it. I had thought of my back yard since she had done such a beautiful job of landscaping it. But I can't very well ask the new owners if I can dig up their yard to bury someone's ashes!"

He laughed. "No. I don't think that would be cool!"

"I haven't had that much experience with these kinds of decisions. I never had any family except for my father, and he's still quite healthy, living in New York. You've had a lot more experience than I have in burying people." She caught herself. "I'm sorry. I didn't mean to sound callous."

"That's okay. You're right. I have had way too much experience with it." Peter was quiet for a minute. "Well, there must be a columbarium in Los Angeles."

"A what?"

"A columbarium."

"What's that?"

"It's a building with niches. People put their ashes in urns in the niches."

"Wow. How did I live all these years not knowing that?"

"Most people haven't heard of them."

"I could look into it. There must be one here."

"That's where Martin's ashes are. The one here in San Francisco is a gorgeous building. And people decorate the niches in incredible ways here. I'm not sure if all columbariums allow that."

Now it was Kate's turn to be silent. "How big are these niches?"

"They have different sizes."

"So more than one urn could be in the larger ones?"

"Yes."

"I'll call you back in a few minutes. I need to talk to Lawrence and his family."

"Okay. I'll be here."

Kate hung up and went back to the living room and spoke to the group. "I think I know what the next step could be."

43

KATE SHARED ALL THE INFORMATION ABOUT THE COLUMBARIUM. Nobody knew about them either. "So I was thinking. Maybe we should take Ruby up to San Francisco and put her in a niche with Martin." She held her breath, worrying if she had overstepped her role and if she had brought up something that might be viewed critically. Would Lawrence be hurt that she thought of this? Would Ruby want to reconcile with her son, so to speak?

"I think that's a fantastic idea! I love it!" exclaimed Lawrence.

Kate exhaled and looked at Michael and Carla. "Yes!" They agreed.

"Okay. I'll call Peter back and get the specifics." She ran back to Ruby's room and Crosby followed, as if to say he, too, agreed. But before she had a chance to press the buttons, her phone rang. It was Finn. "Hi Dad."

"Hi Kate. I'm sorry about Ruby. Was it a heart attack?"

"Yes. It was quick I guess. Hopefully no suffering."

"That's what I hope for."

"Don't talk like that."

"I'm not much younger than Ruby, you know."

"You're healthy. Let's just not go there right now."

"Sorry. So what about Africa?"

"What about it?"

"Will you still go?"

"Of course!" She said it emphatically as if to make it true because, in reality, she didn't feel sure at all. "I just don't know when. Dad? Have you ever heard of a columbarium?"

"Sure. Jed works at the one in San Francisco."

"Jed? You're kidding!"

"Yes. Remember I told you?"

"I remember you told me he had fixed up this building in San Francisco. I guess I just didn't remember what kind of building it was. Well, that's an interesting coincidence."

"Why's that?"

"Martin is buried — is that what you call it — buried?"

"I guess. I don't really know. Maybe interred? Or entombed?"

"Whatever. Anyway, he's in a niche at the one in San Francisco, and we were thinking of putting Ruby with him there."

"I think that's a lovely idea."

"Do you? Oh good. I was hesitant. I thought that might be pushing them on each other."

"For God's sake, Kate, they're dead. It's about what you and Lawrence want to do now."

"You're right. Do you have Jed's phone number?"

"Hold on. I'll look it up." He gave it to her.

"Thanks. I need to call Peter back and then Jed. I'll call you back later, okay?"

"Kate?"

"Yes Dad?"

"You know . . . you don't have to go to Africa."

Why would he say this now? He had always kept quiet about her life choices. That was always something she loved about him when she heard how controlling and judgmental her friends' parents could be. "What do you mean?"

"Just what I said."

"But, what's your point? Why are you saying that?"

"Two reasons. Well, actually, maybe it's one. I'm not getting any younger. Neither are you."

"Huh?" Kate still didn't understand.

"You've finally found love. It's been an awful long time. And I am not going to be around many more years. Being three thousand miles away from my daughter gives me a lot more comfort than being eight thousand miles away."

Kate's mouth dropped. She had never heard her father talk like this. "I don't know what to say."

"Then don't say anything. Just think about what I said. Let me know if there's anything I can do. I love you Kate."

Was this Finn talking? This was not the father she knew. He was gruff and cantankerous and not prone to displays of affection. "I love you too, Dad."

"And say hello to Jed for me."

"I will." She hung up and the tears started again. Everything Finn had said hit way too close to home. Nothing like a death to bring you closer to your own mortality, not just the mortality of the people you love. She took a couple of minutes to compose herself before calling Peter.

"Hi Peter. I think we would like to put Ruby and Martin together in a niche at the San

Francisco Columbarium. And by a truly strange coincidence, I know the man who manages it."

"You're a friend of Jed's?"

"You know Jed too?"

"Everyone knows Jed. Well, everyone that's connected to the columbarium in some way, I guess. He's an amazing person."

Kate smiled, remembering all that had happened with Jed and her father many years ago in Venice. Jed meant so much to Finn. Kate always credited Jed and Mother, for pulling Finn out of a major depression after his wife died. She felt that Jed had helped Finn get past his writer's block and his overindulgence of alcohol. "Yes, Peter. He is an amazing person."

"You seem to surround yourself with some pretty special friends and lovers."

"You mean Martin too, don't you?"

"Yes."

"Well, Martin's brother, Lawrence, isn't too shabby either as amazing people go."

Peter laughed. "You sound like you're a smitten young lady. Am I off base?"

"No. You're not."

"I'm happy for you."

"Thank you." She laughed. "It's a very strange world we live in. Never know what to expect."

"So, what can I do to help?"

"Oh, yes, back to the columbarium. I'll call Jed and get back to you."

"Great. Take care, Kate. I'm sorry about Ruby, but maybe something good has come of all this."

44

KATE LOOKED AT JED'S NUMBER AND WONDERED IF IT WAS A CELL NUMBER OR A HOME PHONE. She couldn't imagine Jed having a cell phone, but that was so long ago. He was obviously leading a very different life than previously when he was homeless on the Venice Beach boardwalk. He had a job now, but it was still hard to imagine how he could afford to live in San Francisco. It was hard to imagine how anyone could afford to live in San Francisco! He might not be able to answer right away if he was at work, so she decided to call and leave a message. She dialed and tried to formulate the message she would leave.

"Hello? Jed Gibbons here."

"Oh. You're there."

"Yes. Hello?"

"Jed. This is Kate. Kate McGee. Finn's daughter."

"Kate! Oh my goodness! What a surprise! Oh God, is Finn —"

"No. He's fine."

"Well, that's good. And how are you?"

"I'm fine, too."

"Finn said you lived about an hour north of San Francisco. I'm sorry. I should have called you."

"Oh, Jed. That's okay. I'm just happy to talk to you now. But actually I'm down in Los Angeles."

"Finn didn't tell me you had moved back."

"I'm not living here. Actually, I don't live anywhere right now." She laughed, thinking about the irony of making that statement to Jed of all people. "There's a lot to talk about but I'd like to talk to you about something specific right now. I'm coming up to San Francisco soon and then we can talk in person and catch up."

"Okay. That sounds good. What's up?"

She took a deep breath, not sure how to begin. "Well . . . I understand you manage the San Francisco Columbarium?"

"I wouldn't say I manage it. I call myself the caretaker."

"Okay. Anyway, my ex-husband, Martin Thomas, has a niche there, and his mother just died and I would like to put her ashes next to Martin's." That was easy! She didn't have to tell the whole story to Jed, at least not now. It was actually a simple request.

"Is he in an apartment or a condo?"

"An apartment?"

"That's what I call the niches. Actually, the bigger ones are called condos."

"That's nice, I like that. But, I don't know what size."

"No problem. I can look it up. Do you know how long he's been here?"

How long has it been since Kate's life changed entirely! Has it been a year? More? Less? "I'm not sure. Let's see . . . I can try to remember."

"That's okay. I can find out. You'll want a condo for two urns, or whatever you choose to put the ashes in. And then, of course, whatever else you might want to put inside. I'll have to look at Martin's and see how much he has in his."

"Wow, Jed. I had no idea. I hadn't even known what a columbarium was before today. And apparently, I still don't know what it is exactly."

Jed laughed. "You're not the only one. Most people don't. I didn't know what a columbarium was either before I started my job here. Would you like me to email you a picture of his apartment?"

Wow. Jed uses a computer and emails too? She couldn't get past the picture of Jed sleeping on the boardwalk with Mother, and his lone backpack. And now he has a job, a cell phone and a computer! "Sure. That would be great." She gave him her email address, and they agreed to talk in a couple of hours.

She went back out to tell Lawrence and the others all that had transpired. It was a much longer story than she had anticipated, because she wanted to explain the relationship between Jed and her father. And that meant going back into her own childhood and Finn's career as a teacher and then best-selling author. That, of course, led to her father's moving in with her after his wife died when she lived in Venice Beach. In order to get into how Finn had met a homeless person on the boardwalk, she felt the need to elaborate on her father's drinking issues.

And they, of course, asked a lot of questions about Jed, because he sounded like such an intriguing person, which he was. His escape from Jonestown fascinated Lawrence, especially. Michael and Carla hadn't lived through those times so they couldn't relate with the same intensity. Most people born after 1980 had very little understanding of the significance of Jonestown, if they were aware of it at all. Mostly, they had only heard that a lot of people committed suicide by drinking Kool-Aid.

After Kate finished they discussed how and when they could all travel to San Francisco. And then there was the inevitable conversation of when Kate would tell the Peace Corps she was available. She couldn't, or rather wouldn't, commit so she let it slide and focused instead on the next couple of days.

She checked her phone often to see if Jed had emailed her the picture, but nothing showed up in the next few hours. Soon it was dinnertime, and they decided to go out. No one felt much like cooking, and there was an air of festivity. Although Ruby had died, they were all there together, and somehow that felt good, not just to Kate and Lawrence, but also to Michael and Carla. That sense of family and belonging was not something any of them had ever experienced to any great extent. Even Danielle had not known a grandmother until Ruby. And death is always, somehow, also a celebration of life.

45

THE CONVERSATION AT DINNER WAS LIVELY AND REVEALING. Since Kate had shared so much about her father, Lawrence did the same. And some of the stories were not even known to Michael. He may have been a crummy father and a lousy boyfriend to Ruby, but he was a fascinating man in his own way. The life of a musician on the road sounded exciting to those not aware of how grueling and tedious it was most of the time. In fact, Kate had gotten so immersed in the conversation that she hadn't called Jed or Peter back.

As soon as they got back to Lawrence's apartment, she opened her laptop and checked her email. There was the picture of Martin's niche, or rather, apartment. It was stark and simple. In the middle was a simple wooden box that probably held his ashes. There were a couple of photographs of him with another man, probably his partner who had also died of AIDS. The only other item was a hand written poem done in beautiful calligraphy. Kate couldn't read the poem easily on the computer screen, but she assumed Martin had written it for the occasion.

Jed had also sent some pictures of several "apartments" and "condos," so that she could get some ideas of how others had chosen to decorate them. "Come look at these," she called to Lawrence who had gone to the bedroom thinking Kate wanted to be alone with her thoughts.

He entered the living room and sat down next to her. "Look at that! This isn't Martin's is it?"

Kate laughed. "Hardly. I don't think he had turned into a cowboy as he aged."

"Are this person's ashes inside the Stetson hat?"

"I guess. And look at the horseshoe and the key ring in the shape of a boot. How about this one? There's a cookie jar shaped like a baseball and a San Francisco Giants pennant." She tried to enlarge the picture. "I can't tell what's on that mural in the back of it. It looks like pictures of people."

"They put a lot of thought into what they want in these niches. Or their friends and family did." Lawrence took Kate's face into his hands and kissed her. "We need to decide what to put in with Ruby's ashes."

"I know." Kate closed her computer. "It's getting late. I'll wait until the morning to call Peter and Jed." She kissed him again. "Let's go to bed."

Kate awoke the next morning to the incessant ringing of her phone. She opened her eyes and saw that Lawrence was already up and out of bed. She looked at the caller id but didn't recognize the number. "Hello?" she asked tentatively.

"Kate McGee?"

"Yes?"

"My name is Joe Halifax. I'm with the Peace Corps office in Washington D.C. I'm sorry if I woke you. Sometimes, I forget about the three hour time difference."

Oh crap! She hadn't decided what to tell them. "Oh, yes. Hello."

"I know this is a difficult time for you. I'm sorry for your loss. But we do need to make plans for your assignment."

"I know. I understand. Honestly, I don't know what to tell you. I just found out that we are going to need to travel to San Francisco —" She stopped herself. She didn't need to tell them everything. "I'm afraid I can't give you a date yet."

"I see. I do need to ask you. Are you in the right frame of mind to make the commitment? I mean you've had a major blow. Losing a parent and all."

She wanted to correct him. Not her own mother, but thought it sounded better to leave him thinking that. And just as she was about to answer him evasively, Lawrence walked in. "Who's that?" he mouthed.

"Excuse me a moment," Kate said into the phone and then covered the phone as she answered Lawrence. "Someone from the Peace Corps office in Washington. I guess they thought they'd take out the big guns to get me to give them a date."

Lawrence shrugged and smiled. "You don't have to go."

"You sound like my father."

"Is that what he said?"

"To my utter shock and amazement, yes. He has never given me any advice like that. It was quite odd."

"Well, how do *you* feel?"

"I am totally confused and torn."

"Then why don't you tell that to the person on the other end of the phone. Just be honest."

"Always the best fallback, isn't it? The truth, that is."

"Yes. Always."

Kate took her hand off the phone. "Mr. Halifax? You are right. I don't know what to tell you because I'm not sure whether I can make that commitment. I feel terrible putting you and all those others in the lurch. I think I'll know better how I feel in a few days and can make a decision. Is that too late?"

"I need to fill the slot you were originally signed up for. But, I will put you on the waiting list and move you to the top for the next position that opens up. Does that sound fair to you?"

"More than fair. But, does that mean it may not be in South Africa?"

"Yes it does mean that. It could be anywhere."

"That will be okay. I appreciate it. Shall I call you in a few days?"

"Yes. Is my number on your phone?"

"Yes. I'll save the contact. Thank you Mr. Halifax."

"Take care and again, my condolences."

She hung up and turned to Lawrence. "He said he had to fill my position but that he would put me at the top of the waiting list. The trouble is it could be anywhere."

"Are you okay with that?"

"Yes. I guess. Anyway, it gives me a few more days to figure it out."

"So does that mean you are thinking of not going?"

"I have no idea. Really I don't. I'd just rather not think about it now. Let's deal with Ruby and the trip to San Francisco. Then, if it's okay with you, I'll come back here and figure it out."

Lawrence grinned broadly. "You bet." He took her in his arms and pulled her back onto the bed.

Kate was on the phone with Peter when Lawrence came out of the shower an hour later. "I've talked to Jed and he's going to move Martin to a larger niche, a condo he calls it. Lawrence and I have to talk to Michael and Carla, but I think we should be able to drive up in the next couple of days. Will you be free to join us at the columbarium when we go there, Peter?"

"Sure. I'll leave my schedule flexible. Just let me know when."

"Thanks Peter. You have certainly—"

"Kate," he interrupted her. "No need to say anything. Martin was a close friend and this is what I want to do."

"Okay. Talk to you soon." She hung up. "All has been worked out on that end. We just have to decide when to go. And I guess we need to find a hotel?"

"Michael and Carla have good friends in San Francisco they can stay with. So just a hotel for us."

"Okay. When do you want to go over to Michael's? Oh, and do we need to pick up the ashes?"

"Let Carla take care of it. She's as good as you are at micromanaging." He grinned.

"Am I micromanaging?"

"It's fine. Not to a detrimental degree. I appreciate it."

She smiled. "That's a relief."

"We can go over in a little while. I have some phone calls to make myself."

"Oh, then I think I'll call my father and let him know that I talked to Jed and will be seeing him."

"He'll like that." Lawrence kissed the top of her head and left the room.

Kate dialed Finn's number. She told him about her conversation with Jed and with Mr. Halifax, and that she may not be going to South Africa. She was surprised that her father hadn't repeated his request for her to stay. She wondered why, but then decided that their last conversation was just a weak, melancholy moment on his part.

46

CARLA WASN'T HOME BUT LAWRENCE HAD A KEY. "Danielle must have gone to preschool today and Carla is picking her up," Lawrence said as he opened the door.

"It's probably good for her to go back to school."

"It's good for both of them. Carla has taken Ruby's death extremely hard."

"They say that getting back to a routine as quickly as possible is important."

Carla and Danielle walked in at that moment, and Danielle ran to Kate and hugged her tightly. Kate hugged her back but looked at Lawrence and Carla, surprised, yet pleased. Kate and Danielle had not developed a particularly close relationship. "Are you going to move in with us now?" Danielle asked.

"Oh sweetie. Remember I told you that Kate is moving far away to Africa for a little while?" Carla said.

Danielle started to whimper. "But I want her to live with us."

Kate hugged her tighter. "I'll visit you and call you."

Carla took Danielle's hand. "Come on. Let's get everyone a snack." They went to the kitchen, but not before Carla pointed to a dark red velvet drawstring bag sitting on a chair and said, "There she is."

Lawrence and Kate looked at each other but didn't speak. The silence lasted a couple of minutes before Kate walked over and picked up the bag. "They're heavier than I thought they would be."

He took the bag from her. "Is this the first time you've felt someone's ashes?"

"Yes. Have you before?"

"No. My wife was buried in a cemetery next to her parents and grandparents. They had a family plot in Illinois. She was from Chicago."

Kate put Ruby's ashes back on the chair. "You haven't told me much about your wife."

"I will in time. There is much more we have to share with each other."

"Yes, I guess there is." Kate squeezed Lawrence's hand.

"Danielle has fixed us a delicious snack of cheese and crackers. Come on in the kitchen," Carla called out.

Michael got home from work about five, and the discussion began on when they would go to San Francisco. After phone calls to their friends in the city and a substitute teacher who Michael liked to use when he had to be absent, they settled on leaving in two days. They would just stay one night and be back by the weekend. Kate thought maybe she could call the Peace Corps and tell them she would be ready for a new assignment starting that Monday, but she secretly hoped they wouldn't have anything for her right away. They had a light dinner. No one was too hungry.

Lawrence and Kate got home fairly early and opened a bottle of wine. "So, what shall we do tomorrow? We have a whole day in Los Angeles with nothing to do. Any thoughts?" Lawrence asked.

"I'd like to go down to Venice. I could show you my old house and hit some of my old haunts."

"That sounds like fun, a relaxing day at the beach."

"I'm not sure how relaxing Venice is, but a walk on the beach would be perfect."

"Very romantic."

Kate smiled. "Sometimes I just have to laugh at this whole turn of events. Who would have ever thought . . ."

"We have some important things to talk about," Lawrence interrupted.

Kate was surprised at his seriousness. "Okay," she answered tentatively. "What do you want to talk about?"

He hesitated before speaking. "You. Us."

Kate fidgeted and took a sip of wine. "What about me and us?" She knew what he meant but was trying to stall for time. She was nervous and didn't know how to answer him.

"I don't want you to go. I know you are an independent woman and will do what you want, but I thought that you should know how I feel. I had even looked into joining you in Africa —"

"You did?"

"Yes. Not in the Peace Corps but just living in Africa and doing some other kind of volunteer work. There are many good organizations where you don't have to go through all the rigmarole that the Peace Corps makes you go through."

"Wow. I don't know what to say."

"I told you that I love you. We're not spring chickens anymore, you know. There's no reason to wait to be together."

"Well, we can continue to plan on being together after I get back."

"Ruby's death . . . well, actually, just connecting with her made me realize the importance of being near all my loved ones. I don't want to leave Michael and his family and I want to be with you. Your father has also voiced his opposition to your being that far away. It would seem that you are the one who could change her plans and make everyone else happy. I know this sounds selfish of me, but I just want to share my thoughts and feelings with you. We will figure out a way to make our relationship work in whatever situation we find ourselves in, and I will continue to love you no matter what you decide." Lawrence took a deep breath and blew it out.

"I'm glad you told me how you felt."

"That was hard for me to do. Thanks for letting me get it all out."

Kate kissed him and fell into his arms. "I am honored and touched and I love you. But I have to think about all of it."

"Of course you do. I didn't expect you to just say 'Oh of course whatever you want!' It was just important for me to say it all so you'd know."

"I hope this isn't disturbing for you to hear, but I need to tell you." Kate hesitated. "When Martin told me he was gay and wanted a divorce, I thought I would never meet anyone who came close to being the incredible man that he was. And I hadn't . . . until you. If I was a religious person, I might say that God was looking out for me or I had some kind of angel on my shoulder."

"But you're not, and I'm not, so let's just say we were lucky to find each other. Many people don't get to find true love even once in their lives. We got to find it twice."

"Well, it's not like either you or I had it easy all these years."

"Then shall we word it differently? We had to go through hard times and much loss so we are the reward for each other?"

"Yes. That sounds better. I wouldn't want anyone to think we had things handed to us on a silver platter!" Kate laughed as she said it.

"No chance of that. So do you want to finish this bottle of wine or go to bed?"

"What do you think?" She stood and pulled him up. "Come on, you."

47

KATE WOKE UP FIRST AND OPENED THE BLINDS. It was warm and sunny, a beautiful day to go to the beach. She looked at Lawrence sleeping and tiptoed out of the room. She wanted time by herself, knowing full well that the more time she spent with Lawrence, the more she would be swayed to staying. She made coffee and went into the living room. "You're up early." She looked up at a yawning Lawrence, entering the room just as she settled into the sofa.

"It's not that early, is it? The sun's pretty bright."

"I guess there is much to learn about each other's habits: waking, sleeping, eating, living . . ."

"We've both lived alone a long time."

"Yes we have." He walked into the kitchen and called out as he poured his coffee, "What time did you want to leave for the beach?"

"I don't know. Um, Lawrence?"

"Yes?" he said as he entered.

"Could I have a little time to myself this morning? I need time to figure out what I want to do about everything we talked about last night."

"Of course. I'll get dressed and go down to my office. I have plenty to catch up on."

"You know, maybe I just need to take a jog. That might be the perfect thing to clear my head." She got up and went back to the bedroom to change into shorts and a T-shirt. "Any suggestions on a route?" she called to him.

"The UCLA running track is just up the hill."

"Off Sunset?"

"Yes."

"I'll find it. Meet you back here in a couple of hours?" Kate came out of the bedroom ready for a run.

"I'll be waiting. Enjoy your run."

"Will you still be going to your office?"

"No. I'll work here."

Kate kissed him goodbye, put her ear buds in and left. She turned on a podcast but decided she should probably put music on. If she listened to a podcast, she would have to pay more attention and then be way too successful at delaying the thought process she was trying to avoid. Normally, she would have listened to rock and roll, something that would enhance the act of running. But this time she turned on some soft jazz.

As she jogged, she weighed the pros and cons, and had discovered even before she got to the running track that there was only one con to her staying. But it was a huge con. It was that she would not be following through with what she thought had been something important to her. She had always wanted to travel. She could still do that with Lawrence. There were many organizations she could work with in Los Angeles that would fulfill her desire to contribute to those less fortunate. The problem was that she would be going back on a commitment she had made to herself. That was the hard part. Sometimes she could be loyal to a fault, to both people and ideals.

Lawrence was dressed and on his computer when Kate got back. "I'll just take a quick shower and then I'll be ready," she said when he opened the door for her.

"Take your time. How was the jog?"

"Excellent."

"Did you make a decision? I'm sorry. I shouldn't pester you. Just tell me what and when you want to. I won't pressure you."

"You're a sweet man. I will tell you when I know. I promise." She kissed him.

They were finally out the door and in his car at ten. It was only a few miles to the beach from his apartment, but in Los Angeles that translated to half an hour. It seemed that the best time one could ever expect to get anywhere in Los Angeles, no matter how many miles away, was thirty minutes, even without much traffic. So, it was ten-thirty when they had parked the car on Venice Boulevard, next to the canals. That was about the closest they were going to get to the beach and not have to pay an arm and a leg for parking. "Do you mind if I take a little nostalgic tour before we step onto the sand?" Kate asked.

"Not at all. I'm happy to follow your lead."

She took him through the canals and then up and down Abbott Kinney Blvd. where they stopped for a large pretzel and coffee to go. Then they hit the walk streets just up from the boardwalk and finally found themselves in front of Kate's old house. She pointed out the different rooms and revealed a personal story for each one. "I loved this house."

"Why don't you knock on the door? Maybe the owners are home and will let you in."

"No. This is fine. I don't mind leaving that part of my life as a memory. Memories are always better than the reality."

"Sometimes worse, but memories are definitely not the reality," Lawrence replied.

"Let's watch the circus on the boardwalk for awhile before a walk on the beach."

"Did you spend a lot of time on the boardwalk when you lived here?"

"No. My father did. That's where he met Jed and a few other fascinating characters."

"There were others?"

"Oh yes. I was working full time and other than a morning jog, I had other things to do with my spare time than hang around this zaniness."

Lawrence laughed. "I look forward to meeting your father."

"If you like Ruby, you'll like Finn. He's just as stubborn and cantankerous."

They strolled, stopping to watch some performers and checking out some arts and crafts tables. They walked by a homeless social services table without giving it much notice. A voice rang out as they were almost past it, "Miss McGee!"

Kate turned around to face a handsome, young black man who looked to be in his late twenties, grinning at her. "Yes?" she replied, but there was no recognition.

"It's Malcolm. Do you remember me? I was in your class at Venice High? A friend of Jed's?"

"Oh my God! Of course! Malcolm!" They hugged. "How are you?"

"I'm fine. How about you? Are you still teaching?"

"Well, I moved to northern California not long after you graduated and taught for awhile up there. I just retired."

"That's wonderful. Did you move back to Venice or just visiting?"

"Visiting," Kate answered quickly. "This is my — uh, Lawrence."

They shook hands. "So, what are you going to do now that you're retired? I can't imagine you'll be sitting in your house watching soap operas."

"No, definitely not her style," Lawrence smiled. He looked at Kate, curious how she would answer.

"I haven't decided yet." She winked at Lawrence, knowing full well that he wanted to see how she'd answer. "So, what else have you been doing besides this volunteering?" She hoped that's what he was doing, just volunteering at the homeless table rather than partaking of its offerings.

"I did a stint in the army and learned some engineering stuff. I had a couple of jobs at the Department of Veterans Affairs before I got an Associates degree in Video Production at

Santa Monica College. Then I interned and worked at a couple of television stations."

"That's cool. What did you do at the TV stations?"

"Mostly cameraman."

"Did you enjoy it?"

"It was okay. I do a lot of volunteering here and also at the children's cancer hospital. That's where my heart is. Actually I want to write a book and I'm trying to find time for that."

She was proud that he had come so far, after the awful circumstances he had been in, but wondered why he used the past tense and if he was once again living on the streets. She wanted to ask, really wanted to help him, but thought maybe she shouldn't pry so she changed the subject. "I'm actually going to see Jed tomorrow. He lives in San Francisco now."

"Are you? Oh wow. I'd love to see him. Do you have his phone number?"

"Sure." Kate looked on her phone. Malcolm took out his phone and added the contact. "And let's exchange numbers, too."

Lawrence started to open his mouth to say that he ought to know that he may be calling Africa or some other faraway place, and it might cost a little more than he wanted to spend, but then thought he should let Kate tell him that. "It's really nice to see you, Miss McGee."

"You can call me Kate now that I'm not your teacher anymore."

"Okay . . . Kate." Malcolm grinned again, but then his face got serious. "Miss Ruthie died a couple of years ago."

"Oh, I'm sorry to hear that. So, who is taking care of those babies now, I wonder."

"There are some volunteers continuing her good work." He smiled.

Of course! Miss Ruthie probably left Malcolm her house since she had eventually adopted him. He had a place to live! "Well, how far along are you in your book?"

"Not very far, I'm afraid. You taught me really well but it hasn't translated into getting me past a writer's block."

"My father had many serious bouts of writer's block and he published a few books so don't despair."

"I forgot that your father was a writer."

"I'd get you in touch with him, but he lives in New York."

"Oh, that's too bad."

Some kids approached the table and Malcolm went to talk to them. "He seems like a special kid," Lawrence said after they said their goodbyes.

"His mother died when he was about fourteen, and that left him homeless. Jed had befriended him on the boardwalk and got him a place to live in Miss Ruthie's home. She used to take in babies of addicts, who needed rocking to soothe them and get them off the drugs that their mothers had passed on to them. Jed used to go there and rock them also."

"How strange to run into him the day before you will be seeing Jed after all these years."

"There's probably some magical reason, I guess."

"You think?"

Kate shrugged. "Maybe it's all somehow connected to Ruby's death."

"How New Age of you!"

Kate punched his arm playfully. "Let's go walk on the beach and get all romantic and stuff."

48

THEY SPENT THE REST OF THE DAY ON THE BEACH AND WENT OUT FOR AN EARLY DINNER. "What time shall we leave in the morning?" Kate asked as they finished paying the bill. "I told Peter I'd text him a ballpark time so he would be available to meet us at the columbarium."

"It's about a six hour drive, so why not tell him about three. I'll tell Carla and Michael to plan to leave by nine."

"Oh, we're not driving together?"

"I thought it best if we drove separately. They have to be back the following day, and we don't know what we might want to do. Right?"

"Sure. I need to pick up some things before we leave. Do you mind if I borrow your car?"

"What do you need?"

"I want it to be a surprise." He looked at her quizzically. She smiled.

"Sure. Just drop me off at home." Lawrence drove while Kate took out her phone to text Peter. She noticed there were a few voice mails from Peter, Jed and Joe Halifax. The ones from Peter and Jed were what she expected: just asking around what time they expected to get there. The one from Joe Halifax was not expected. The place where she had originally been assigned was particularly excited about having Kate. They felt she was perfect for what they needed so they were holding it for her. Just what she needed, another addition to the muddle that the decision-making process had become. She chose not to share this with Lawrence. That would only make it harder.

He pulled up in front of his building and kissed her before getting out of the car. "How long do you think you'll be? Should I wait up for you?"

"You're kidding right? I'll be back in an hour."

"Yes. I was just kidding. Take as long as you need." He left and Kate slid into the driver's seat.

She took Beverly Glen to the Valley and arrived at Michael and Carla's about twenty minutes later. "I hope you don't mind me coming. I just need to get a couple of things from Ruby's room," she told Carla when she opened the door.

"Sure. What did you need?"

"I kind of want it to be a surprise. And would you mind not telling Lawrence that I was here?"

"Okay. No problem."

Kate went into Ruby's room and got what she wanted. She hugged Carla and left hurriedly, before Michael and Danielle even knew she was there. She made one more stop at Home Depot and was in Lawrence's living room before the hour was up. They went straight to bed, knowing that they may not have that many more nights together.

They were on the road before eight the next morning, which was probably not such a good idea since rush hour was in full swing, but they were eager to get there. They took Interstate 5 because it was an hour shorter than the 101, although much less picturesque. There were a couple of Starbucks en route, so they could stop every couple of hours and that made the six-hour drive less tedious. They purposely waited until they got to the Bay area before grabbing lunch so they had a better choice of restaurants.

Peter arrived just as they pulled into the parking lot of the columbarium. Michael and his family drove up a few minutes later. After hugs and introductions and a fair amount of marveling at the beauty of the building, they went inside to find Jed.

The outside of the columbarium doesn't even come close to the magnificence of the inside. They were all speechless and wide-eyed; even Peter who had been there many times, said he still experienced an enormous sense of awe every time he walked inside. In fact, they were all so mesmerized that they didn't notice Jed approaching. "Kate?"

She turned around to see that familiar, smiling face filled with serenity and wisdom and remembered why her father had been so taken with this man. His background was so fascinating that he became the subject of the book Finn had been writing at the time, and they also became close friends. "Jed!" She hugged him and was surprised when her eyes filled with tears. She had no idea why, other than it must be that melancholy one feels when reliving a memory.

Jed gave them a tour, highlighting some of his favorite niches. They marveled at the creativity and individuality people used to decorate their "apartments" and "condos." He brought them to Martin's, and they were all silent when it dawned on them the significance of what was happening.

There was the reunification of Martin and Ruby after so many years of estrangement. There was the fact that they were saying goodbye to Ruby who had become the matriarch of this family in just a few short months. There was the fact that Lawrence was "meeting" his twin brother for the first time. There was the umbrella of death that hung over the building, even though it felt like a warm, happy place full of love. And for Kate and Lawrence, there was the realization that being here meant that the task that had brought Kate back to Los Angeles was finished, and she would be free to leave.

"Did you bring anything to put in the condo along with the ashes?" Jed asked.

Michael and Carla looked at Kate and Lawrence, unsure how to respond. "Yes," Kate answered, much to the others' relief.

Carla brought out the wooden box that the crematorium had given her and gave it to Jed. "Here are Ruby's ashes. Maybe we should have thought of another container to put them in, one that would be more personal."

"I brought some things that will make it special to Ruby." She opened her purse and took out a guitar pick, a packet of seeds and knitting needles.

Lawrence hugged her and smiled. "So that's what you needed the car for last night."

"I wish I had some pictures of all of you to add as well but all I have is a picture of Crosby."

"Why don't you put Crosby with her," Michael said. Then he turned to Jed. "Can we add to the niche, I mean condo, at a later date?"

"Of course," Jed answered as he placed the ashes inside and nodded to Kate to add her items to it. "And you know, I promise to watch over her and talk to her everyday. I see by the guitar pick that she was musical. I have a few people that I sing to every morning. What kind of music does she like?"

They looked at each other and spoke in unison, "Blues."

"Any particular song?" Jed asked. They shrugged their shoulders. "I know "Tain't Nobody's Bizness if I Do" if you think that would be appropriate."

They laughed. "Absolutely. That would be perfect. Ruby and Bessie Smith had much in common," Kate replied.

"Did you have a service of some kind that you wanted to have?"

"No. We agreed no service. None of us are particularly religious."

"It doesn't have to be religious," Jed replied.

"I think we just want to say goodbye to Ruby and be on our way. It was a long drive and we need to check in to our hotel." Lawrence looked at Kate to see if she agreed. She nodded.

Jed looked at his watch. "Would you mind waiting for a couple of minutes? Monica wanted to meet you and she will be here shortly."

"Monica?" Kate asked.

"My wife."

Kate's eyes bugged out so far, Lawrence thought they were going to pop out of their sockets. "I didn't know! Does my father know you're married?"

"He didn't tell you?"

"No."

Jed smiled. "Maybe he didn't believe it either."

"I'm afraid I really must go," Peter chimed in. "But it was great seeing you again, Kate, and meeting the rest of Martin's family." He hugged Kate, said goodbye to the group, and left.

"You'll never guess who I ran into on the boardwalk yesterday," Kate said to Jed.

"Malcolm?"

"How did you know?"

"He called me last night. You gave him my number, didn't you?"

"That's right. I did. Isn't it wonderful how well he's doing?"

"Makes me proud."

"And he's even continuing to rock the babies."

"Yes."

"Do you miss that?"

"I do it here at the hospital. I volunteer a couple of days a week."

Just as Kate was about to answer, a beautiful woman approached them. It was hard to figure out how old she was and what race or ethnicity she was, but she was stunning. "Sorry I'm late."

Jed put his arm around her. "Monica, I want you to meet Kate, Finn's daughter. And this is Lawrence, Michael, Carla and Danielle."

"It's wonderful to meet you all." She turned to Kate. "I've heard so much about you and your father."

"My father and Jed had a special relationship. When was the last time you saw him, Jed?"

"It's been quite a few years, but we talk periodically."

"I wish I could stay, but I must get back to work. I just wanted to meet the daughter of the man who saved my husband's life." Monica kissed Jed on the cheek and left.

Kate looked at Jed and smiled. "I always thought it was the other way around."

"Maybe we both saved each other."

Kate turned to Carla and asked, "What do you think Danielle understands about what we are doing here?"

Carla shrugged. "I'm not sure. I tried to explain it to her."

Kate handed the picture of Crosby to Danielle. "Would you like to put Crosby next to Ruby?"

"Where's Ruby?" Danielle asked.

"In the box," Kate answered.

"Is Crosby dead too?" Danielle looked like she was going to cry.

Kate hugged her. "No, sweetie. He's waiting for you at home. But he wanted to be close to Ruby too."

"I want to be close to her too!" Danielle started to cry.

"Wait. I have a picture of Danielle in my wallet!" Carla shuffled through her purse and took the picture out of its plastic casing. "Here, honey, put your picture and Crosby's picture next to the box." She gave her the picture.

Danielle looked at her picture. She stopped crying and sniffled a couple of times. Then she smiled. "This is when we went to Disneyland for my birthday." She put the picture inside, leaning against the box. She put the photo of Crosby next to the box on the other side.

"Now you can both be near Ruby all the time," Kate said. She stepped back and looked at the condo. She wanted to say something but decided she would rather just walk away. Maybe

she'd come back someday and talk to both
Martin and Ruby, tell them how she had felt all
those years ago and how she feels now. But this
wasn't the time for that. She had way too much
sorting out to do. "I think I'll wait in the car.
Take your time." Kate turned around abruptly
and left, unsure if her tears and sobs were for
Ruby or for all that had gone before. Or was it
fear and anxiety over the difficult future-altering
decisions that lay ahead.

49

KATE AND LAWRENCE CHECKED IN TO THE HOTEL. "I have a little work to do before dinner," Lawrence said.

"Work? Oh, okay."

"I need to check on a few things."

"I think I'll go out for a jog, then. I need some thinking time, anyway."

"Shall we plan on dinner at seven?"

"Perfect." She changed into her running clothes, kissed him, and left.

The hotel was an old Victorian inn on Stanyan, across the street from Golden Gate Park. She felt safe, since it wouldn't be dark for another hour or so and the inn was in Cole Valley, just south of Haight-Ashbury. Cole Valley was more of a residential neighborhood, not prone to the tourists and seediness of the Haight. And jogging in the park would make it easy for her to ruminate without worrying about traffic and pedestrians. She could find a path away from the museums and flower gardens, so she could let her mind wander into whatever places she would let it. And that is exactly what she did.

It was interesting that Ruby's death seemed to take a back seat at this point. Maybe it was just that since the interment into the columbarium was over, the grieving would last awhile longer. She thought a bit about Martin, and then Malcolm and Jed, but she didn't dwell on them, either. They were doing something important and compassionate with their lives. That's what she had always wanted to do. She had done that by becoming a teacher, but the Peace Corps would be a much bigger "making-a-difference" activity. She would be working to give an education to adolescent girls who didn't normally have access to one. It was something she felt strongly about. In some of these countries fewer than ten percent of girls are able to go to school. Sure there were plenty of opportunities here to help people and change lives, but she had wanted to go in the Peace Corps for so long.

What she hadn't counted on happening was meeting and falling in love with Lawrence. She'd been alone for so long and gotten so used to it, that she had stopped looking for love. Being in the columbarium certainly brought death and her father's mortality to the surface, as well as her own. If she didn't stay and take this opportunity to be with Lawrence, she may lose it. Something could happen to one of them. Or he might meet someone else. She started to run harder. The harder she pounded the surface, the more her frustration and fear became pronounced. She had hoped that this jog would bring serenity and get her closer to making a decision. But it seemed to make her fear, frustration, and apprehension more pronounced. She knew deep down that those feelings were all part of the process, but knowing that didn't make it any easier to go through.

Her father had always told her that the best thing to do when you didn't know what to do was to do nothing. But what was the status quo? She didn't really know. She had no home. She laughed loudly. She was just like Malcolm, Jed, and even Finn. All three of them had experienced homelessness at one time. Maybe she wasn't living on the streets or the Venice Beach boardwalk, but home wasn't just having a roof over one's head. It was comfort, security, safety . . . even freedom in a way. She had always thought freedom was not being tethered to one place, but maybe she was wrong.

She glanced at her watch and saw that she had been running for an hour. She needed to get back to the hotel to shower and dress and be ready by seven. She sighed. She felt no closer to making a decision.

Lawrence wasn't in the room when she got back, but he arrived while she was in the shower and was waiting for her when she emerged from the bathroom. "I'll be ready in a few minutes."

"No problem. I made a reservation for seven-fifteen at the French bistro down the street."

"Sounds delicious. I'm actually starving. We didn't eat much today."

"We'll make up for it tonight." She got dressed and they were there in time for their reservation.

Dinner was filled with wine, delicious food, reminiscing about Ruby, personal stories from their childhoods, and an animated discussion comparing the virtues and downsides of San Francisco and Los Angeles. Whenever San Francisco was touted as the obvious winner in such a comparison, it inevitably came down to weather, giving Los Angeles the edge. But the conversation never touched on their future. That is, until dessert when Lawrence put a small box on the table.

"What's that?" Kate asked.

"It's a very inexpensive symbol for what I want to say."

"Huh?"

"I know you wouldn't want me to spend money on this, so I found a tourist trap on Haight Street."

"What are you talking about?"

He opened the box and took out a ring with a turquoise stone and a design on the band. "It's not exactly a diamond, but I didn't think you'd want that." Kate's mouth dropped and she didn't speak. "Whatever you decide to do now, I want it to be as my wife. If you stay or if you go . . . either way."

And then Kate laughed. Lawrence looked hurt and bewildered. He wasn't sure what Kate's answer would have been, but he hadn't expected her to laugh. She kissed him and said, "I'm sorry. I'm just surprised . . . more like flabbergasted. I was only laughing at how your last sentence was a song lyric."

He relaxed and smiled. "Oh."

She took the ring and placed it on her finger. "It's perfect." Then she turned to him and kissed him on the lips. "Yes. I will marry you."

"I thought we could either stop at City Hall here or do it back in Los Angeles. Or we could go to Vegas or Reno if you're in a hurry to leave."

"I don't think I want to write in my memoir that I was married in Las Vegas or Reno," Kate said.

"Me neither. We're here now. What do you think?"

"Like tomorrow?"

"Yes. Like tomorrow."

Kate burst out laughing and Lawrence soon joined in. "This is crazy," Kate said.

50

THEY WENT TO SAN FRANCISCO CITY HALL AT NINE THE NEXT MORNING. They had gotten lucky. Although getting a marriage license and getting married were by appointment only, they were able to go online the night before, and there were openings for both. The Office of the County Clerk opened at eight but the reservation for the license wasn't until nine. They had to wait until one to get married, but that wasn't really much of an inconvenience. They had called Michael and he, Carla, and Danielle were perfectly happy to change their plans and leave after the ceremony. They would meet them for an early lunch and then they would go together to the Deputy County Commissioner's office. They figured they'd be on the road by two and would still get home to Los Angeles at a reasonable hour. Kate debated about inviting Jed as a stand-in for her father, but decided not to. It just didn't seem right since Finn couldn't be there.

She had called Finn early that morning and given him all the news. He was thrilled and had asked the inevitable question about what she was going to do about the Peace Corps. She had made a decision but thought it only fair that she told Lawrence first. She wasn't planning to tell him until they got back to his apartment that night. So she put Finn off, telling him that she hadn't decided. His last words were that he would like to come to California for a visit soon to see her and meet Lawrence and his family, and also to see Jed. He asked her to please let him know as soon as possible, so he could plan his trip. She swallowed hard and hung up before she allowed any of those tears to flow, tears that were coming far too often these days.

They got the license quickly and easily, although neither of them could remember the dates that their previous marriages had legally ended. Luckily they had a savvy clerk who indicated that no one would be checking, so they wrote dates that seemed correct. The whole process took half an hour, so they had a couple of hours to kill before meeting up with Michael and his family.

City Hall wasn't too far from the Castro where Martin's apartment had been. Lawrence wanted to see it. That was as close as he would ever be to meeting the brother he never knew he had. He thought it would fill some kind of gap that he wasn't even sure needed filling. But since Martin had been a part of Kate's life too, not to mention Ruby's, it just seemed appropriate.

Danielle was beside herself with excitement at the whole idea of a wedding. Carla tried to explain to her that this was not going to be anything like weddings she had seen in books and movies. The bride was not going to be wearing a white dress with a long veil. There would not be bridesmaids and ushers and a slew of well-wishers. Carla and Michael did stop at a florist on the way to the restaurant, however, and brought a bouquet for Kate to carry and flowers for Danielle to hold, so she could pretend that she was a flower girl. They had also bought her a stuffed cat, so she could pretend that Crosby was there too. She couldn't manage to hold both the flowers and the cat, so poor Michael had to feel silly carrying a stuffed animal at his father's wedding ceremony.

They were on the road by two, perfect timing. They didn't have to leave San Francisco at rush hour and they would get to Los Angeles after rush hour was over. They decided to take the 101 going home. It was a little longer but much prettier since it hugged the coastline for most of the trip.

There was not a lot of conversation. Both Kate and Lawrence seemed to want the silence and the time to think about what they had just done and what lay ahead. But it was a comfortable silence, filled with the warmth, contentment and trust that is the signature of love between two people.

51

THEY STOPPED FOR DINNER IN SANTA BARBARA SO BY THE TIME THEY GOT BACK TO LAWRENCE'S, IT WAS TIME FOR BED. They managed to keep the conversation light and playful throughout dinner and kept up the flirtatious banter for the hour and a half from Santa Barbara to Los Angeles. By the time they crawled into bed, they were quite ready to consummate their marriage. And neither one had brought up anything to do with the looming decision that Kate had to make. Both of them knew that it was important to keep this day precious and intimate.

But the next morning was a different story. The ringing of Kate's phone woke them up and when she looked at the caller's number, she knew it was time. "Hello? Yes. Hi, Mr. Halifax." She looked over at Lawrence's eyes staring at her with a combination of fear, love, hope and curious anticipation. She took a deep breath. "I'll get back to you in a couple of hours. I promise. Thanks." She hung up and got out of bed without a word or a glance at

Lawrence. She hurried into the bathroom and closed the door.

Lawrence wasn't sure how to interpret that, but decided to get up and make breakfast. Kate was dressed in running clothes when she entered the kitchen. "Do you mind if we wait to eat? I'd like to take a quick jog first."

"That's fine. I didn't start the eggs yet. Are you sure you wouldn't like some coffee first, at least?"

"No thanks." She kissed him and left.

Lawrence's mind went to a million places, trying to figure out what Kate was doing. But he was good at compartmentalizing and knew that Kate was not. He could put aside the random thoughts in his mind and not let them overrun it. She needed to gather data, let her mind wander and obsess, before putting it together and come to a conclusion.

And he was right about Kate. That's exactly what she was doing. But what he didn't realize is that she had actually already reached a decision, and was using this hour-long jog to make sure. She also needed to remind herself that she could change her mind either way. Nothing was written in stone. As soon as she remembered that, she turned around abruptly and ran back to Lawrence's.

She entered his apartment, breathless, and rushed to his desk where he sat typing on the computer. She hugged him tightly and he reciprocated. "Well, that was a nice greeting!" he said.

"Can you take a break now? I'm starving!"

"Sure. Do you want to shower and get dressed while I make breakfast?"

"Why? Do I smell?" she teased as she sniffed under her arms.

"I love the way you smell."

"Well, that was a clever way to get out of it!" She smiled and hit his arm playfully. "I'll be ready in fifteen minutes." She bustled out of the room.

She seemed so cheerful that Lawrence couldn't help but think that she had decided to stay. He found himself humming and whistling as he made breakfast.

They sat down at the table to eggs, toast, fruit and coffee and ate quietly for a few minutes. Lawrence had already decided to let her talk first. After she had poured both of them another cup of coffee, she finally did.

"I'm going to go."

He pursed his lips and didn't even try to hide his disappointment. He didn't answer right away. He just sighed, shrugged his shoulders, and waited for her to continue.

"First, I'm going to make sure that I can change my mind and leave anytime if I want.

They say that in the literature they put out, but I want to check." Lawrence still didn't answer her. "I know this is not what you wanted. Or probably what you expected. Are you angry?"

"No." He finally spoke. "Just sorry that you're leaving. But it's your decision, and if that's what you want, I support it."

"Thank you. Do you understand why?"

"Sort of."

"I can come back and visit you in a few months. And I thought maybe after you retire next year, you could join me there. I know there are things you could be doing. You could work with one of the agencies that work with the Peace Corps, and then you wouldn't have to go through the rigmarole of applying and all." He looked at her skeptically. She shrugged. "Or not."

"I'll be okay, Kate. If that's what you need to do. Or what you want to do. I get it."

"Thanks for understanding. I love you. That has nothing to do —"

He touched her arm gently. "No need to explain. Honestly."

"Are you surprised?"

"Yes. I guess I assumed that since you agreed to marry that you wanted to stay. But it doesn't change anything. I'll retire, and we can decide what we want to do after that happens and then again after you come back. Have you told your father?"

"Not yet. He won't be happy about it either. Nothing like having the two most important people in my life disappointed in me."

"We're not disappointed in you. We're just disappointed. You have to understand the difference. I'm sure he agrees with me that it is a noble and valuable thing that you are doing."

"Ruby said that to me too," Kate added.

"That's right. I remember that she did. Why don't you call your father and Mr. Halifax back, and then we can make some plans for our last couple of days together."

She kissed him and stood up. "You are one extraordinary man and I am one very lucky lady."

"We may not end up where we thought we were going but we'll always end up where we are meant to be. I remember reading that somewhere," Lawrence said.

"Yeah, I seem to recall that something similar was said once by John Lennon."

Lawrence smiled. "Man plans and God laughs."

Read an excerpt from Emily Gallo's next novel:
THE ROAD NOT TAKEN

1

THE CLOUDS STARTED TO ROLL IN, OBSCURING THE SUN. The chill of late afternoon on the beach forced the sun-worshippers to fold up their chairs and blankets. Malcolm took out his phone to check the time. Charlie promised he'd be back to the table by four so Malcolm would have enough time to shower and dress before he had to be at the restaurant. It was a Monday in March so the boardwalk wasn't teeming with tourists. And neither had college spring breaks started yet, so he didn't have to put up with the students' drunken raillery.

"Sorry I'm late," a breathless Charlie rushed up to the table. "We had an emergency at the center."

"No problem. It's okay. What was the emergency?"

"Belligerent husband threatening his frightened wife and kids. So what else is new, right?"

Malcolm shook his head. "Did you have to call the cops?"

"Oh, yeah. That was the only way we could get him to leave. She had a restraining order but he didn't seem to think it pertained to him even though it had his name on it."

"Did they take him in?"

"For now. We're trying to find a safe house for the wife and kids."

"I better go so I won't be late for work."

"Hey, thanks Malcolm. You're a godsend. Couldn't do this without you."

Malcolm waved and jogged off. He got home with enough time for a quick shower and he was at the restaurant by five to start his shift. Waiting tables was not his career choice, but it gave him enough to get by until he could figure out whatever the hell his career choice was. He thanked Miss Ruthie everyday for leaving him her house and that it had been paid for years before he moved into it. Coming up with the taxes and insurance payments a couple of times a year was difficult, but not having to pay rent gave him much needed breathing room. And Venice Beach was a pretty good place to live when you were a Black man in his late twenties with no family to rely on.

To say his childhood had been difficult would be an understatement. He was born in Texas and he and his mother had spent his first fourteen years fleeing from his abusive father. It was the typical story: poverty coupled with alcohol turning into anger and violence, and the son trying to protect his mother and then becoming the target. They moved continually to hide from him and eventually cut off all contact with his mother's family so that his father could not torture them to get information. They lived in Arizona and New Mexico before finally landing in California.

Just when it seemed that they could breathe easy and perhaps lead a normal life, his mother got cancer and was dead within a year. Before becoming too sick to get out of bed, she had worked as a card dealer in a poker club in Inglewood. She had made enough for a one-room apartment in the Oakwood section of Venice, an area not known for being a trendy, gentrified section catering to tourists and hipsters. It was considered the "ghetto" of Venice although it was still hard to find an apartment under a thousand dollars a month, no matter what the square feet.

Malcolm was fourteen when his mother died. She had finally gone into a coma and spent her last couple of months in the hospital. Malcolm had lived alone in the apartment until the landlord found out and then he was sleeping on the boardwalk. His mother had spent her whole life keeping him from that fate, always finding a place to stay. Luckily, she had never known that he had ended up there. And lucky for him, he didn't stay there long, thanks to the homeless resource table he now volunteered at. And thanks to Miss Ruthie who took him in as a foster child and eventually adopted him and whose house he now owned. And thanks to Jed, a man who touched so many people's lives besides his.

Malcolm had returned to Venice when Miss Ruthie became sick. He was used to caretaking a dying mother and he was good at it. His army stint was over by then. It was time to go to school since he had money to pay for it from the GI Bill. He could take classes and still nurse Miss Ruthie. She had already found people willing to take the babies into their homes so Malcolm could devote his time to his studies and to her.

Miss Ruthie had been famous in Los Angeles for taking in newborns of drug-addicted mothers. She had been written up in the Times and even been interviewed on television for her work. Miss Ruthie took the babies home, and recruited volunteers to help her rock them to quiet their screaming and get them to sleep.

She had been doing this for many years and had gotten enough grant money and private donations to buy her house. She had started taking in difficult to place foster children as well and had a one hundred percent success rate at finding permanent homes for all her children. Until she met Malcolm, that is. He was the only one she had adopted herself. Not because he would have necessarily been hard to place. They just had a special bond from the beginning and she knew that if she were ever to have had her own child, it would have been someone like Malcolm.

A retired teacher, Emily Gallo also dabbles in screenwriting, blues piano and portrait drawing. She cofounded The Derelict Voice, a writing workshop for the homeless. "Kate & Ruby" is her third novel. Born and raised in Manhattan, she and her husband now divide their time between two and a half acres in northern California and 750 square feet on the beach in southern California.

www.ingramcontent.com/pod-product-compliance
Lightning Source LLC
Chambersburg PA
CBHW051637180726
48284CB00006B/1765